Miriam Coles Harris

Richard Vandermarck

A Novel

Miriam Coles Harris

Richard Vandermarck
A Novel

ISBN/EAN: 9783337001162

Printed in Europe, USA, Canada, Australia, Japan

Cover: Foto ©Andreas Hilbeck / pixelio.de

More available books at **www.hansebooks.com**

RICHARD VANDERMARCK.

A NOVEL.

By Mrs. SIDNEY S. HARRIS,

AUTHOR OF "RUTLEDGE," "ST. PHILLIPS,"
ETC., ETC.

NEW YORK:
CHARLES SCRIBNER & COMPANY.
1871.

To S. S. II.

CONTENTS.

RICHARD VANDERMARCK.

CHAPTER I.

VARICK STREET.

O for one spot of living green,
 One little spot where leaves can grow,—
To love unblamed, to walk unseen,
 To dream above, to sleep below !

Holmes.

There are in this loud stunning tide,
 Of human care and crime,
With whom the melodies abide
 Of th' everlasting chime ;

*   *   *   *   *

And to wise hearts this certain hope is given ;
" No mist that man may raise, shall hide the eye of Heaven."

Keble.

I NEVER knew exactly how the invitation came ; I
felt very much honored by it, though I think now,
very likely the honor was felt to be upon the other
side. I was exceedingly young, and exceedingly
ignorant, not seventeen, and an orphan, living in the

house of an uncle, an unmarried man of nearly seventy, wholly absorbed in business, and not much more interested in me than in his clerks and servants.

I had come under his protection, a little girl of two years old, and had been in his house ever since. I had had as good care as a very ordinary class of servants could give me, and was supplied with some one to teach me, and had as much money to spend as was good for me—perhaps more; and I do not feel inclined to say my uncle did not do his duty, for I do not think he knew of anything further to do; and strictly speaking, I had no claim on him, for I was only a great-niece, and there were those living who were more nearly related to me, and who were abundantly able to provide for me, if they had been willing to do it.

When I came in to the household, its wants were attended to by a cook and a man-servant, who had lived many years with my uncle. A third person was employed as my nurse, and a great deal of quarrelling was the result of her coming. I quite wonder my uncle did not put me away at board somewhere, rather than be disturbed. But in truth, I do not believe that the quarrelling disturbed him much, or that he paid much attention to the matter, and so the matter settled itself. My nurses were changed very often, by will of the cook and old Peter, and I never was happy enough to have one who had very high principle, or was more than ordinarily good-tempered.

I don't know who selected my teachers; probably they applied for employment and were received. They were very business-like and unsuggestive people. I was of no more interest to them than a bale of goods, I believe. Indeed, I seemed likely to go a bale of goods through life; everything that was done for me was done for money, and with a view to the benefit of the person serving me. I was not sent to school, which was a very great pity; it was owing to the fact, no doubt, that somebody applied to my uncle to teach me at home, and so the system was inaugurated, and never received a second thought, and I went on being taught at home till I was seventeen.

The "home" was as follows; a large dark house on the unsunny side of a dull street; furniture that had not been chang° for forty years, walls that were seldom repainted, windows that were rarely opened. The neighborhood had been for many years unfashionable and undesirable, and, by the time I was grown up, nobody would have lived in it, who had cared to have a cheerful home, I might almost have said, a respectable one. I fancy ours was nearly the only house in the block occupied by its owner; the others,

1*

equally large, were rented for tenement houses, or
boarding-houses, and perhaps for many things worse.
It was probably owing to this fact, that my uncle
gave orders, once for all, I was never to go into the
street alone; and I believe, in my whole life, I had
never taken a walk unaccompanied by a servant, or
one of my teachers.

A very dull life indeed. I wonder how I endured
it. The rooms were so dismal, the windows so uneventful. If it had not been for a room in the garret
where I had my playthings, and where the sun came
all day long, I am sure I should have been a much
worse and more unhappy child. As I grew older, I
tried to adorn my room (my own respectable sleeping
room, I mean), with engravings, and the little ornaments that I could buy. But it was a hopeless attempt. The walls were so high and so dingy, the
little pictures were lost upon them; and the vases on
the great black mantel-shelf looked so insignificant, I
felt ashamed of them, and owned the unfitness of
decorating such a room. No flowers would grow in
those cold north windows—no bird would sing in
sight of such a street. I gave it up with a sigh; and
there was one good instinct lost.

When I was about eleven, I fell foul of some good
books. If it had not been for them, I truly do not

see how I could have known that I was not to lie or
steal, and that God was to be worshipped. Certainly,
I had had my hands slapped many times for taking
things I had been forbidden to touch, and had had
many a battle in consequence of "telling stories,"
with the servants of the house, but I had always
recognized the personal spite of the punishments, and
they had not carried with them any moral lesson.

I had sometimes gone to church ; but the sermons
in large city churches are not generally elementary,
and I did not understand those that I heard at all.
Occasionally I went with the nurse to Vespers, and
that I thought delightful. I was enraptured with the
pictures, the music, the rich clothes of the priests; if
it had not been for the bad odor of the neighboring
worshippers, I think I might have rushed into the
bosom of the Church of Rome. But that offended
sense restrained me. And so, as I said, if I had not
obtained access to some books of holy and pure influence, and been starved by the dullness of the life
around me into taking hold of them with eagerness,
I should have led the life of a little heathen in the
midst of light. Of course the books were not written
for my especial case, nor were they books for children,
—and so, much was supposed, and not expressed, and
consequently the truth they imparted to me was but

fragmentary. But it was truth, and the influence
was holy.

I was driven to books; I do not believe I had any
more desire than most vivid, palpitating, fluttering
young things of my sex, to pore over a dull black and
white page; but this black and white gate opened to
me golden fields of happiness, while I was perishing
of hunger in a life of dreary fact.

When I was about sixteen, however, an outside
human influence, not written in black and white,
came into the current of my existence. About that
time, my uncle took into his firm, as junior partner, a
young man who had long been a clerk in the house.
After his promotion he often came home with my uncle
to dinner. I think this was done, perhaps, with a view
of civil treatment, on the first occasion; but afterward, it was continued because my uncle could not
bear to leave business when he left the office, and because he could talk on the matters which were dearer
to him than his dinner, with this junior, in whom he
took unqualified delight. He often wrote letters in
the evening, which my uncle dictated, and he sometimes did not go away till eleven o'clock at night.
The first time he came, I did not notice him very
much. It was not unusual for Uncle Leonard to be
accompanied by some gentleman who talked business

with him during dinner; and being naturally shy, and moreover, on this occasion, in the middle of a very interesting book, at once timid and indifferent, I slipped away from the table the moment that I could. But upon the third or fourth occasion of his being there, I became interested, finding often a pair of handsome eyes fixed on me, and being occasionally addressed and made a partner in the conversation. Uncle Leonard very rarely talked to me, and I think found me in the way when Richard Vandermarck made the talk extend to me.

But this was the beginning of a very much improved era for me. I lost my shyness, and my fear of Uncle Leonard, and indeed, I think, my frantic thirst for books, and became quite a young lady. We were great friends; he brought me books, he told me about other people, he opened a thousand doors of interest and pleasure to me. I never can enumerate all I owed to him. My dull life was changed, and the house owed him gratitude.

We began to have the gas lighted in the parlor, and even Uncle Leonard came in there sometimes and sat after dinner, before he went up into that dreary library above. I think he rather enjoyed hearing us talk gayly across his sombre board; he certainly became softer and more human toward me after Richard came to be so constantly a guest. He gave me more money to spend, (that was always the expression of his feelings, his language, so to speak;) he made various inquiries and improvements about the house. The · dinners themselves were improved, for a horrible monotony had crept into the soups and sauces of forty years; and Uncle Leonard was no epicure; he seemed to have no more stomach than he had heart; brain and pocket made the man.

I think unconsciously he was much influenced by Richard, whose business talent had charmed him, and to whom he looked for much that he knew he must soon lose. He was glad to make the house seem pleasant to him, and he was much gratified by his frequent coming. And Richard was peculiarly a man to like and to lean upon. Not in any way brilliant, and with no literary tastes, he was well educated enough, and very well informed; a thorough business man. I think he was ordinarily reserved, but our intercourse had been so unconventional, that I did not think him so at all. He was rather good-looking, tall and square-shouldered, with light-brown hair and fine dark-blue eyes; he had a great many points of advantage.

One day, long after he had become almost a member of the household, he told me he wanted me to know his sister, and that she would come the next day to see me, if I would like it. I did like it, and waited for her with impatience. He had told me a great deal about her, and I was full of curiosity to see her. She was a little older than Richard, and the only sister; very pretty, and quite a person of consequence in society. She had made an unfortunate marriage, though of that Richard said very little to me; but with better luck than attends most unfortunately-married women, she was released by her husband's early death, and was free to be happy again, with some pretty boys, a moderate fortune, and two brothers to look after her investments, and do her little errands for her. She considered herself fortunate; and was a widow of rare discretion, in that she was wedded to her unexpected independence, and never intended to be wedded to anything or anybody else. She was naturally cool and calculating, and was in no danger of being betrayed by her feelings into any other course of life than the one she had marked out as most expedient. If she was worldly, she was also useful, intelligent, and popular, and a paragon in her brother's partial eyes.

CHAPTER II.

Mieux vaut une once de fortune qu'une livre de sagesse.

AT last (on the day on which Richard had advertised me she was coming,) the door was opened, and some one was taken to the parlor. Then old Peter rang a bell which stood on the hall table, and called out to Ann Coddle (once my nurse, now the seamstress, chambermaid, and general lightener of his toils), to tell Miss Pauline a lady wanted her.

This bell was to save his old bones; he never went up-stairs, and he resented every visitor as an innovation. They were so few, his temper was not much tried. I was leaning over the stairs when the bell rang, and did not need a second message. Ann, who continued to feel a care for my personal appearance, followed me to the landing-place and gave my sash a last pull.

When I found myself in the parlor I began to experience a little embarrassment. Mrs. Hollenbeck was so pretty and her dress was so dainty, the dingy, stiff, old parlor filled me with dismay. Fortunately, I did not think much of myself or my own dress.

But after a little, she put me at ease, that is, drew me out and made me feel like talking to her.

I admired her very much, but I did not feel any of the affection and quick cordiality with which Richard had inspired me. I could tell that she was curious about me, and was watching me attentively, and though she was so charming that I felt flattered by her interest, I was not pleased when I remembered my interview with her.

"You are not at all like your brother," I said, glancing in her face with frankness.

"No?" she said smilingly, and looking attentively at me with an expression which I did not understand.

And then she drew me on to speak of all his features, which I did with the utmost candor, showing great knowledge of the subject.

"And you," she said, "you do not look at all as I supposed. You are not nearly so young—Richard told me you were quite a child. I was not prepared for this grace; this young ladyhood—'cette taille de palmier,'" she added, with a little sweep of the hand.

Somehow I was not pleased to feel that Richard had talked of me to her, though I liked it that he had talked of her to me. No doubt she saw it, for I was lamentably transparent. "Do you lead a quiet life, or have you many friends?" she said, as if she did not know exactly the kind of life I led, and as if she had not come for the express purpose of helping me out of it, at the instance of her kindly brother. Then, of course, I told her all about my dull days, and she pitied me, and said lightly it must not be, and I must see more of the world, and she, for her part, must know me better, etc., etc. And then she went away.

In a few days, I went with Ann Coddle, in a carriage, to return the visit. The house was small, but in a beautiful, bright street, and the one window near the door was full of ferns and ivies. I did not get in, which was a disappointment to me, particularly as I had no printed card, and realized keenly all the ignominy of leaving one in writing. This was in April, and I saw no more of my new friend. Richard was away, on some business of the firm, and the days were very dull indeed.

In May he came back, and resumed the dinners, and the evenings in the parlor, though not quite with the frequency of the past winter,—and I think there was the least shade of constraint in his manner. It was on one of these May days that he came and took me to the Park. It was a great occasion; I had never been so happy before in my life. I was in great doubt about taking Ann Coddle; never having been out of the house without a person of that description in attendance before. But Ann got a suspicion of my doubt and settled it, to go—of course. I think Richard was rather chagrined when she followed us out to get into the carriage; she was so dried-up and shrewish-looking, and wore such an Irish bonnet. But she preserved a discreet silence, and looked stead-fastly out of the carriage window, so we soon forgot that she was there, though she was directly opposite to us. It was Saturday; the day was fresh and lovely, and there were crowds of people driving in the Park. Once we left the carriage with Ann Coddle in it, and went to hear the music. It was while we were sit-ting for a few moments under the vines to listen to it, and watch the gay groups of people around us, that a carriage passed within a dozen feet, and a lady leaned out and bowed with smiles.

"Why, see—it is your sister!" I exclaimed, with the vivacity of a person of a very limited acquaint-ance.

"Ah," he said, and raised his hat carelessly. But I saw he was not pleased; he pushed the end of his moustache into his mouth, and bit it, as he always did when 'out of humor, and very soon proposed we should go back and find the carriage. It was not long, however, before he recovered from this annoy-ance, as he had from the unexpected pleasure of Ann's company; and, I am sure, was as sorry as I when it was time to go home to dinner.

He stayed and dined with us; another gentleman had come home with my uncle, who talked well and amused us very much. I was excited and in high spirits; altogether, it was a very happy day.

It was more than a week after this, that the invitation came which turned the world upside down at once, and made me most extravagantly happy. It was from Mrs. Hollenbeck, and I was asked to spend part of June and all of July and August, with them at R——.

At R—— was their old family home, a place of very little pretension, but to which they were much attached. When the father died, five years before, the two sons had bought the place, or rather had taken it as their share, turning over the more productive property to their sister.

They had been very reluctant to close the house, and it was decided that Sophie should go there every summer, and take her servants from the city; the expenses of the place being borne by the two young men. They were very well able to do it, as both were successful in business, and keeping open the old home, with no diminution of the hospitality of their father's time, was perhaps the greatest pleasure that they had. It was an arrangement which suited Sophie admirably. It gave her the opportunity to entertain pleasantly and informally; it was a capital summer-home for her two boys; it was in the centre of an agreeable neighborhood; and above all, it gave her yearly-exhausted purse time to recuperate and swell again before the winter's drain. Of course she loved the place, too, but not with the simple affection that her two brothers did. The young men invited their friends there without restriction, as was to be supposed; and Sophie was a gay and agreeable hostess. No one could have made the house pleasanter than she did; and she left nothing undone to gratify her brothers' tastes and wishes, like a wise and prudent woman as she was.

I did not know all this then, or my invitation might not have overwhelmed me with such gratitude to her. I reproached myself for not having loved her the first time I saw her.

Three months! Three happy months in the country! I could hardly believe it possible such a thing had happened to me. I took the note to my uncle without much fear of his opposition, for he rarely opposed anything that I had the courage to ask him, except going in the street alone. (I believe my mother had made a runaway match, and I think he had faith

in inherited traits; his one resolution regarding me
must have been, not to give me a chance.) He read
the note carefully, and then looked me over with
more interest than usual, and told me I might go.
Afterward he gave me a roll of bills, and told me to
come to him for more money, if I needed it.

I was much excited about my clothes. I could not
think that anything was good enough to go to R——;
and I am afraid I spent a good deal of my uncle's
money. Ann Coddle and the cook thought that my
dresses were magnificent, and old Peter groaned over
the coming of the packages. I had indeed a wardrobe
fit for a young princess, and in very good taste besides,
because I was born with that. An inheritance, no
doubt. And my uncle never complained at all about the
bills. I seemed to have become, in some way, a person of considerable importance in the house. Ann
Coddle no more fretted at me, but waited on me with
alacrity. The cook ceased to bully me, and on the
contrary, flattered me outrageously. I remembered
the long years of bullying, and put no faith in her
assurances. I did not know exactly why this change
had happened, but supposed it might be the result of
having become a young lady, and being invited to pay
visits.

CHAPTER III.

KILIAN.

You are well made—have common sense,
And do not want for impudence.

Faust.

Tanto buen che val niente.

Un sot trouve toujours un plus sot qui l'admire.

THE packages finally ceased coming and the stiff
old bell from being pulled; but only half an hour before the carriage drove to the door that was to take
me to the boat. Ann Coddle was flying up and down
the stairs, and calling messages over to Peter in a
shrill voice. She was not designed by nature for a
lady's maid, and was a very disagreeable person to
have about one's room. She made me even more
nervous than I should otherwise have been. I had
never packed a trunk before, or had one packed, and
might have thought it a very simple piece of business
if Ann had not made such a mountain of it; packing
every tray half a dozen times over, and going down-
stairs three times about every article that was to come
up from the laundry.

Happily she was not to go with me any farther than the boat. Richard was away again on business —had been gone, indeed, since the day after we had driven in the Park: so I was to be put on board the boat, and left in charge of Kilian, his younger brother, who had called at my uncle's office, and made the arrangement with him. I had never seen Kilian, and the meeting filled me with apprehension; my uncle, however, sent up one of his clerks in the carriage to take me to the boat, and put me in charge of this young gentleman. This considerate action on the part of my uncle seemed to fill up the measure of my surprises.

When we reached the boat, the clerk, a respectful youth, conducted me to the upper deck, and then left me with Ann, while he went down about the baggage.

With all our precautions, we were rather late, for the last bell was ringing; Ann was in a fever of impatience, and I was quite uncertain what to do, the clerk not having returned, and Mr. Kilian Vandermarck not having yet appeared. Ann was so disagreeable, and so disturbing to all thinking, that I had more than once to tell her to be quiet. Matters seemed to have reached a crisis. The man at the gangway was shouting "all aboard;" the whistle was blowing; the bell was ringing; Ann was whimpering; when a belated-looking young man with a book and paper under his arm came up the stairs hurriedly and looked around with anxiety. As soon as his eye fell on us, he looked relieved, and walked directly up to me, and called me by name, interrogatively.

" O yes," I said eagerly, " but do get this woman off the boat or we'll have to take her with us." " Oh, no danger," he said, " plenty of time," and he took her toward the stairs, at the head of which she was met by the clerk, who touched his hat to me, handed the checks to Mr. Vandermarck, then hurried off with Ann. Mr. Vandermarck returned to me, but I was so engrossed looking over the side of the boat and watching for Ann and the clerk, that I took no notice of him.

At last I saw Ann scramble on the wharf, just before the plank was drawn in ; with a sigh of relief I turned away.

" I want to apologize for being so late," he said.

" Why, it is not any matter," I answered, " only I had not the least idea what to do."

" You are not used to travelling alone, then, I suppose ?"

" Oh no," nor to travelling any way, for the matter of that, I added to myself; but not aloud, for I had a great fear that it should be known how very limited my experience was.

" You must let me take your shawl and bag, and we

2

will go and get a comfortable seat," he said in a few
moments. We went forward and found comfortable
chairs under an awning, and where there was a fine
breeze. It was a warm afternoon, and the change
from the heated and glaring wharf was delightful.
Mr. Vandermarck threw himself back in his chair with
an expression of relief, and took off his straw hat.

"If you had been in Wall-street since ten o'clock
this morning you would be prepared to enjoy this
sail," he said.

"Is Wall-street so very much more disagreeable
than other places? I think my uncle regrets every
moment that he spends away from it."

"Ah, yes. Mr. Greer may; he has a good deal to
make him like it; if I made as much money as he
does every day there, I think it's possible I might like
it too. But it is a different matter with a poor devil
like me: if I get off without being cheated out of all
I've got, it is as much as I can ask."

"Well, perhaps when he was your age, Uncle
Leonard did not ask more than that."

"Not he; he began, long before he was as old as I
am, to do what I can never learn to do, Miss d'Estrée—
make money with one hand and save it with the
other. Now, I'm ashamed to say, a great deal of
money comes into my pockets, but it never stays

there long enough to give me the feeling that I'm a rich man. One gets into a way of living that's destruction to all chances of a fortune."

"But what's the good of a fortune if you don't enjoy it?" I said, thinking of the dreary house in Varick-street.

"No good," he said. "It isn't in my nature to be satisfied with the knowledge that I've got enough to make me happy locked up somewhere in a safe: I must get it out, and strew it around in sight in the shape of horses, pictures, nice rooms, and good things to eat, before I can make up my mind that the money is good for anything. Now as to Richard, he is just the other way: old head on young shoulders, old pockets in young breeches (only there ar'nt any holes in them). He's a model of prudence, is my brother Richard. *Qui garde son dîner, il a mieux à souper.* He'll be a rich man one of these fine days. I look to him to keep me out of jail. You know Richard very well, I believe?" he said, turning a sudden look on me, which would have been very disconcerting to an older person, or one more acquainted with the world.

"O, very well indeed," I said with great simplicity. "You know he is such a favorite with my uncle, and he is a great deal at the house."

" Well he may be a favorite, for he is built exactly on his model; at seventy, if I am not hung for debt before I reach it, I shall look to see him just a second Mr. Leonard Greer."

I made a gesture of dissent. "I don't think he is in the least like Uncle Leonard, and I don't think he cares at all for money."

"O, Miss Pauline, don't you believe him if he says he doesn't. I'm his younger brother, whom he has lectured and been hard on for these twenty-seven years, and I know more about it than anybody else."

" Why, is Mr. Richard Vandermarck twenty-seven years old?" I said with much surprise.

"Twenty-nine his next birthday, and I am twenty-seven. Why, did he pass himself off for younger? That's an excellent thing against him."

"No; he did not pass himself off for anything in the matter of age. It was only my idea about him. I thought he was not more than twenty-five, perhaps even younger than that. But then I had nobody but Uncle Leonard to compare him with, and it isn't strange that I didn't get quite right."

" It *is* something of a step from Mr. Greer to Richard, I must say. Mr. Greer seems so much the oldest man in the world, and Richard—well, Richard isn't that, but he is a good deal older than he ought to be. But do you tell me, Miss Pauline, you havn't any younger fellows than Richard on your cards? Do they keep you as quiet as all that in Varick-street?"

I knew by intuition this was impertinence, and no doubt I looked annoyed, and Mr. Vandermarck hastened to obliterate the impression by a very rapid movement upon the scenery, the beauties of the river, and many things as novel.

The three hours of our sail passed away pleasantly. Mr. Vandermarck did not move from his seat; did not even read his paper, though I gave him an opportunity by turning over the leaves of my "Littel" on the occurrence of every pause.

I felt that I knew him quite well before the journey was over, and I liked him exceedingly, almost as well as Richard. He was rather handsomer than Richard, not so tall, but more vivacious and more amusing, much more so. I began to think Richard rather dull when I contrasted him with his brother.

When we reached the wharf, Mr. Vandermarck, after disposing of the baggage, gave his arm to me, and took me to an open wagon which was waiting for us. He put me in the seat beside him, and took the reins with a look of pleasure.

"These are Tom and Jerry, Miss Pauline," he said, "about the pleasantest members of the family; at least they contribute more to my pleasure than any other members of it. I squandered about half my income on them a year or two ago, and have not repented yet; though, indeed, repentance isn't in my way. I shall hope for the happiness of giving you many drives with them, if I am permitted."

"Nothing could make me happier, I am sure."

"Richard hasn't any horses, though he can afford it much better than I can. He does his driving, when he is here, with the carriage-horses that we keep for Sophie—a dull old pair of brutes. He disapproves very much of Tom and Jerry; but you see it would never do to have two such wise heads in one family."

"It would destroy the balance of power in the neighborhood."

"Decidedly; as it is, we are a first-class power, owing to Sophie's cleverness and Richard's prudence; my prodigality is just needed to keep us from overrunning the county and proclaiming an empire at the next town meeting. How do you like Sophie, Miss d'Estrée? I know you haven't seen much of her—but what you have? Isn't she clever, and isn't she a pretty woman to be nearly thirty-five?"

I was feeling very grateful for my invitation, and

so I said a great deal of my admiration for his sister.

"Everybody likes her," he said, complacently. "I don't know a more popular person anywhere. She is the life of the neighborhood; people come to her for everything, if they want to get a new door-mat for the school-house, or if they want a new man nominated for the legislature. I think she's awfully bored, sometimes, but she keeps it to herself. But though the summer is her rest, she always does enough to tire out anybody else. Now, for instance, she is going to have three young ladies with her for the next two months (besides yourself, Miss d'Estrée), whom she will have to be amusing all the time, and some friends of mine who will turn the house inside out. But Sophie never grumbles."

"Tell me about them all," I said, consuming with a fever of curiosity.

"O, I forgot you did not know them. Shall I begin with the young ladies?—(Sam, there's a stone in Jerry's off fore-foot; get down and look about it—Steady!—there, I knew it)—Excuse me, Miss d'Estrée. Well,—the young ladies. There's one of our cousins, a grand, handsome, sombre, estimable girl, whom nobody ever flirts with, but whom somebody will marry. That's Henrietta Palmer.

were hideous. I should not have been afraid of young or old men, nor of old women; but they were just my age, just my class, just my equals, or ought to have been, if I had had any other fate than Uncle Leonard and Varick-street. How they would criticize me! How soon they would find out I had never been anywhere before! I wished for Richard then with all my heart. Kilian had already deserted me, and was talking to Miss Leighton, who had come half-way down the steps to meet him, and who only gave me a glance and a very pretty smile and nod, when Mrs. Hollenbeck presented me to them. Miss Benson and Miss Palmer each gave me a hand, and looked me over horribly; and the tones of their voices, when they spoke to me, were so constrained and cold, and so different from the tones in which they addressed each other. I hated them.

After a few moments of wretchedness, Sophie proposed to take me to my room. We went up the stairs, which were steep and old-fashioned, with a landing-place almost like a little room. My room was in a wing of the house, over the dining-room, and the windows looked out on the river. It was not large, but was very pretty. The windows were curtained, and the bed was dainty, and the little mantel was draped, and the ornaments and pictures were quaint and delightful to my taste.

Sophie laid the shawls she had been carrying up for me upon the bed, and said she hoped I would find everything I needed, and would try to feel entirely at home, and not hesitate to ask for anything that would make me comfortable.

Nothing could be kinder, but my affection and gratitude were fast dying out, and I was quite sure of one thing, namely, that I never should love Sophie if she spent her life in inviting me to pay her visits. She told me that tea would be ready in half an hour, and then left me. I sat down on the bed when she was gone, and wished myself back in Varick-street; and then cried, to think that I should be homesick for such a dreary home. But the appetites and affections common to humanity had not been left out of my heart, though I had been beggared all my life in regard to most of them. I could have loved a mother so—a sister—I could have had such happy feelings for a place that I could have felt was home. What matter, if I could not even remember the smile on my mother's lips; what matter, if no brother or sister had ever been born to me; if no house had ever been my rightful home? I was hungry for them all the same. And these first glimpses of the happy lives of others seemed to disaffect me more than ever with my own.

CHAPTER IV.

"Vous êtes belle : ainsi donc la moitié
Du genre humain sera votre ennemie."
Voltaire.

" Oh, I think the cause
Of much was, they forgot no crowd
Makes up for parents in their shroud."
R. Browning.

THE servant came to call me down to tea while I
was still sitting with my face in my hands upon the
bed. I started up, lit the candles on the dressing-
table, arranged my hair, washed the tears off my face,
and hurried down the stairs. They were waiting for
me in the parlor, and no doubt were quite impatient,
as they had already waited for the arrival of the evening train, and it was nearly eight o'clock. The evening train had brought Mr. Eugene Whitney, of whom
I can only say, that he was a very insignificant young
man indeed. We all moved into the dining-room;
the others took the seats they were accustomed to.
Mr. Whitney and I, being the only new-comers, were

advised which seats belonged to us by a trim young
maid-servant, and I, for one, was very glad to get into
mine. Mr. Whitney was my neighbor on one hand,
the youngest of the Hollenbeck boys on the other.
These were our seats:

Kilian,

Miss Leighton,	Miss Henrietta Palmer,
Miss Benson,	Mr. Eugene Whitney,
Tutor,	Myself,
Boy,	Boy,

Mrs. Hollenbeck.

The seat opposite me was not filled when we sat
down.

"Where is Mr. Langenau, Charley?" said his
mother.

"I'm sure I don't know, mamma," said Charley,
applying himself to marmalade.

"Charley doesn't see much of his tutor out of hours,
I think," said Miss Benson.

"A good deal too much of him in 'em," murmured
Charley, between a spoonful of marmalade and a drink
of milk.

"Benny's the boy that loves his book," said Kilian;
"he's the joy of his tutor's heart, I know," at which
there was a general laugh, and Benny, the younger,
looked up with a merry smile.

The Hollenbeck boys were not fond of study. They were healthy and pretty; quite the reverse of intellectual; very fair and rosy, without much resemblance to their mother or her brothers. It was evident the acquisition of knowledge was far from being the principal pursuit of their lives, and the tutor was looked upon as the natural enemy of Charley, at the least.

"I don't see what you ever got him for, mamma," said Charley. "I'd study just as much without him."

"And that wouldn't be pledging yourself to very much, would it, Charley dear?"

"Wish he was back in Germany with his ugly books," cried Charley.

But—hush!—there was a sudden lull, as the tutor entered and took his place by Charley. He was a well-made man, evidently about thirty. He was so decidedly a gentleman, in manners and appearance, that even these spoiled boys treated him respectfully, and the young ladies and gentlemen at the table were more stiff than offensive in their manner. But he was so evidently not one of them!

It is very disagreeable to be among people who know each other very well, even if they try to know you very well and admit you to their friendship. But

I had no assurance that any one was trying to do this
for *me*, and I am afraid I showed very little inclination to be admitted to their friendship. I could not
talk, and I did not want to be talked to. I was even
afraid of the little boys, and thought all the time that
Charley was watching me and making signs about me
to his brother, when in reality he was only telegraphing about the marmalade.

In the meantime, without any attention to my feelings, the business of the tea-table proceeded. Mrs.
Hollenbeck poured out tea, and kept the little boys
under a moderate control. Kilian cut up some birds
before him, and tried to persuade the young ladies to
eat some, but nobody had appetite enough but Mr.
Whitney and himself. Charlotte Benson, who was
clever and efficient and exceedingly at home, cut up a
cake that was before her, and gave the boys some
strawberries, and offered some to me. Miss Palmer
simply looked very handsome, and eat a biscuit or
two, and tried to talk to Mr. Whitney, who seemed to
have a good appetite and very little conversation.
Miss Leighton gave herself up to attentions to Kilian;
she was saying silly little things to him in a little low
tone all the time, and offering him different articles
before her, and advising him what he ought to eat; all
of which seemed most interesting and important in

dumb-show till you heard what it was all about, and then you felt ashamed of them. At times, I think, Kilian felt somewhat ashamed too, and tried to talk a little to the others; but most of the time he seemed to like it very well, and did not ask anything better than the excellent woodcock on his plate, and the pretty young woman by his side.

"By the way," said Sophie, when the meal was nearly over, "I had a letter from Richard to-day."

"Ah!" said Kilian, with a momentary release from his admirer. "And when is he coming home?"

I looked up with quick interest, and met Mrs. Hollenbeck's eyes, which seemed to be always on me. Then I turned mine down the table uncomfortably, and found Charlotte Benson looking at me too. I did not know what I had done to be looked at, but wished they would look at themselves and let me take my tea (or leave it alone) in peace.

"Not for two weeks yet," said his sister; "not for two whole weeks."

"How sorry I am," said Charlotte Benson.

"I think we are all sorry," said Henrietta the tranquil.

"Miss d'Estrée confided to me that she'd be glad to see him," said Kilian, cutting up another woodcock and looking at his plate.

"Indeed I shall," I said, with a little sigh, not thinking so much about them as feeling most earnestly what a difference his coming would make, and how sure I should be of having at least one friend when he got here.

"He seems to be having a delightful time," said his sister.

"I am glad to hear that," I said, interested. "Generally he finds it such a bore. He doesn't seem to like to travel." I was rather startled at the sound of my own voice and the attention of my audience; but I had been betrayed into speaking, by my interest in the subject, and my surprise at hearing he was having such a pleasant time.

"Ah!" she said, "don't you think he does? At any rate, he seems to be enjoying this journey, and to be in no hurry to come back. I looked for him last week."

Warned by my last experience, I said nothing in answer; and after a moment Kilian said:

"Well, if Richard's having a good time, you may be sure he's made some favorable negotiation, and comes home with good news for the firm. That's his idea of a good time, you know."

"Ah!" said Sophie, gently, "that's his brother's idea of his idea. It isn't mine."

Charlotte Benson seemed a little nettled at this, and exclaimed,

"Mrs. Hollenbeck ! you are making us all unhappy. You are leading us to suspect that the stern man of business is unbending. What's the influence at work ? What makes this journey different from other journeys ? Where does he tarry, oh, where ?"

"Nonsense !" said Sophie, with a little laugh. "You cannot say I have implied anything of the sort. Cannot Richard enjoy a journey without your censure or suspicion ? You must be careful; he does not fancy teasing."

"O, I shall not accuse him, you may be sure; that is, if he ever comes. Do you believe he really ever will ?"

"Not if he thinks you want him," said Kilian, amiably. "He has a great aversion to being made much of."

"Yes, a family trait," interrupted Charlotte, at which everybody laughed, no one more cordially than Miss Leighton.

"Leave off laughing at my Uncle Richard," said Benny, stoutly, with his cheeks quite flushed.

"We have, dear, and are laughing at your Uncle Kilian. You don't object to that, I'm sure," and Charlotte Benson leaned forward and threw him a little kiss past the tutor, who wore a silent, abstracted look, in odd contrast with the animated expressions of the faces all around him.

Benny did not like the joke at all, and got down from his chair and walked away without permission. We all followed him, going into the hall, and from thence to the piazza, as the night was fine. The tutor walked silently through the group in the hall to a seat where lay his book and hat, then passed through the doorway and disappeared from sight.

CHAPTER V.

And now above them pours a wondrous voice,
(Such as Greek reapers heard in Sicily),
With wounding rapture in it, like love's arrows.

George Eliot.

THE next day, the first of my visit, was a very sultry one, and the rest of the party thought it was, no doubt, a very dull one.

Kilian and Mr. Eugene Whitney went away in the early train, not to return, alas, till the evening of the following day. Miss Leighton was languid, and yawned incessantly, though she tried to appear interested in things, and was very attentive to me. Charlotte Benson and Henrietta laid strong-minded plans for the day, and carried them out faithfully. First, they played a game of croquet, under umbrellas, for the sun was blazing on the ground: that was for exercise; then, for mental discipline, they read history for an hour in the library; and then, for relaxation, under veils and sunhats, read Ruskin for two hours by the river.

I cannot think Henrietta understood Ruskin, but I

have no doubt she thought she did, and tried to share
in her friend's enthusiasm. Sophie had a little headache, and spent much of the morning in her room.
The boys were away with their tutor in the farm-
house where they had their school-room, and the
house seemed deserted and delightful. I wandered
about at ease, chose my book, and sat for hours in the
boat-house by the river, not reading Ruskin, nor even
my poor little novel, but gazing and dreaming and
wondering. It can be imagined what the country
seemed to me, in beautiful summer weather, after the
dreary years I had spent in a city-street.

It is quite impossible to describe all that seemed
starting into life within me, all at once—so many
new forces, so much new life.

My home-sickness had passed away, and I was inclined to be very happy, particularly in the liberty
that seemed to promise. Dinner was very quiet, and
every one seemed dull, even Charlotte Benson, who
ordinarily had life enough for all. The boys were
there, but their tutor had gone away on a long walk
and would not be back till evening. "*A la bonne
heure*," cried Madame, with a little yawn; "freedom
of the halls, and deshabille, for one afternoon."

So we spent the afternoon with our doors open, and
with books, or without books, on the bed.

Nobody came into my room, except Mrs. Hollenbeck for a few moments, looking very pretty in a white peignoir, and rather sleepy at the same time; hoping I was comfortable and had found something to amuse me in the library.

It seemed to be thought a great bore to dress, to judge from the exclamations of ennui which I heard in the hall, as six o'clock approached, and the young ladies wandered into each other's room and bewailed the necessity. I think Miss Leighton would have been very glad to have stayed on the bed, and tried to sleep away the hours that presented no amusement ; but Charlotte Benson laughed at her so cruelly, that she began to dress at once, and said, she had not intended what she said, of course.

I was the first to be ready, and went down to the piazza. The heat of the day was over and there was a soft, pleasant breeze. We were to have tea at seven o'clock, and while I sat there, the bell rang. The tutor came in from under the trees where he had been reading, looking rather pale after his long walk.

He bowed slightly as he passed me, and waited at the other end of the piazza, reading as he stood, till the others came down to the dining-room. As we were seating ourselves he came in and took his place, with a bow to me and the others. Mrs. Hollenbeck asked him a little about his expedition, and paid him a little more attention than usual, being the only man.

He had a most fortunate way of saying just the right thing and then being silent; never speaking unless addressed, and then conveying exactly the impression he desired. I think he must have appeared in a more interesting light that usual at this meal, for as we went out from the dining-room Mary Leighton put her arm through mine and whispered "Poor fellow! How lonely he must be! Let's ask him to go and walk with us this evening."

Before I could remonstrate or detach myself from her, she had twisted herself about, in a peculiarly supple and child-like manner that she had, and had made the suggestion to him.

He was immeasurably surprised, no doubt, but he gave no sign of it. After a silence of two or three instants, during which, I think, he was occupied in trying to find a way to decline, he assented very sedately.

Charlotte Benson and her friend, who were behind us, were enraged at this proceeding. During the week they had all been in the house together, they had never gone beyond speaking terms with the tutor, and this they had agreed was the best way to keep things, and it seemed to be his wish no less than

theirs. Here was this saucy girl, in want of amusement, upsetting all their plans. They shortly declined to go to walk with us : and so Mary Leighton,
Mr. Langenau, and I started alone toward the river.

It must be confessed, Miss Leighton was not re-
warded for her effort, for a stiffer and more uncomfortable companion could not be imagined. He
entirely declined to respond to her coquetry, and she
very soon found she must abandon this rôle; but she
was nothing if not coquettish, and the conversation
flagged uncomfortably. Before we reached home
she was quite impatient, and ran up the steps, when
we got there, as if it were a great relief. The tutor
raised his hat when he left us at the door, turned
back, and disappeared for the rest of the evening.

The next morning, coming down-stairs half an hour
before breakfast, I went into the library (a little room
at the right of the front door), for a book I had left
there. I threw myself into an easy-chair, and opened
it, when I caught sight of the tutor, reading at the
window. I half started to my feet, and then sank
back again in confusion; for what was there to go
away for?

He rose and bowed, and resumed his seat and his
book.

The room was quite small, and we were very near

each other. How I could possibly have missed seeing him as I entered, now surprised me. I longed to go away, but did not dare do anything that would seem rude. He appeared very much engrossed with his book, but I, for my part, could not read a word, and was only thinking how I could get away. Possibly he guessed at my embarrassment, for after about ten minutes he arose, and coming up to the table by which I sat, he took up a card, and placed it in his book for a mark, and shut it up, then made some remark to me about the day.

The color was coming and going in my face.

He must have felt sorry or curious, for he did not go directly away, and continued to talk of things that did not require me to answer him.

I do not know what it was about his voice that was so different from the ordinary voices of people. There was a quality in it that I had never heard in any other. But perhaps it was in the ear that listened, as well as the voice that spoke. And apart from the tones, the words I never could forget. The most trivial things that he ever said to me, I can remember to this day.

I believe that this was not of my imagination, but that others felt it in some degree as I did. It was this that made him such an invaluable teacher; he

3

impressed upon those flesh-and-blood boys, in that
one summer, more than they would have learned in
whole years from ordinary persons. It was not very
strange, then, that I was smitten with the strangest
interest in all he said and did, and that his words
made the deepest impression on me.

No doubt it is pleasant to be listened to by one
whose face tells you you are understood; and the
tutor was not in a hurry to go away. He had got up
from the window, I know, with the intention of going
out of the room, but he continued standing, looking
down at me and talking, for half an hour at least.

The soft morning wind came in at the open door
and window, with a scent of rose and honeysuckle:
the pretty little room was full of the early sunshine
in which there is no glare : I can see it all now, and I
can hear, as ever, his low voice.

He talked of the book I held in my hand, of the
views on the river, of the pleasantness of country life.
I fancy I did not say much, though I never am able
to remember what I said when talking to him.
Whatever I said was a mere involuntary accord with
him. I never recollect to have felt that I did not
agree with and admire every word he uttered.

How different his manner from last night when he
had talked with Mary Leighton ; all the stiffness, the

half-concealed repelling tone was gone. I had not heard him speak to any one, except perhaps once to Benny, as he spoke now. I was quite sure that he liked me, and that he did not class me with the others in the house. But when the breakfast-bell rang, he gave a slight start, and his voice changed; and such a frown came over his face! He looked at his watch, said something about the hour, and quickly left the room. I bent my head over my book and sat still, till I heard them all come down and go into the breakfast-room. I trusted they would not know he had been talking to me, and there was little danger, unless they guessed it from my cheeks being so aflame.

At breakfast he was more silent than ever, and his brow had not quite got over that sudden frown. At dinner he was away again, as the day before.

The day passed much as yesterday had done. About four o'clock there came a telegram from Kilian to his sister. He had been delayed, and Mr. Whitney would wait for him, and they would come the next evening by the boat. I think Mary Leighton could have cried if she had not been ashamed. Her pretty blue organdie was on the bed ready to put on. It went back into the wardrobe very quickly, and she came down to tea in a gray barége that was a little shabby. .

A rain had come on about six o'clock. At tea the candles were lit, and the windows closed. Every one looked moped and dull ; the evening promised to be insufferable. Mrs. Hollenbeck saw the necessity of rousing herself and providing us some amusement. When Mr. Langenau entered, she met his bow with one of her best smiles : how the change must have struck him ; for she had been very mechanical and polite to him before. Now she spoke to him with the charming manner that brought every one to her feet.

And what was the cause of this sudden kindness? It is very easy for me to see now, though then I had not a suspicion. Alas ! I am afraid that the cheeks aflame at breakfast-time were the immediate cause of the change. Mrs. Hollenbeck would not have made so marked a movement for an evening's entertainment : it seemed to suit her very well that I should talk to the tutor in the library before breakfast, and she meant to give me opportunities for talking to him in the parlor too.

" A dreary evening, is it not? she began." " What " shall we all do? Charlotte, can't you think of something?"

Charlotte, who had her own plans for a quiet evening by the lamp with a new book, of course could not think of anything.

"Henrietta, at least you shall give us some music, and Mr. Langenau, I am sure you will be good enough to help us; I will send over to the school-room for that flute and those piles of music that I've seen upon a shelf, and you will be charitable enough to play for us."

" I must beg you will not take that trouble."

" Oh, Mr. Langenau, that is selfish now."

Mrs. Hollenbeck did not press the subject then, but made herself thoroughly delightful during tea, and as we rose from the table renewed the request in a low tone to Mr. Langenau : and the result was, a little after eight o'clock he came into the parlor where we sat. A place was made for him at the table around which we were sitting, and Mrs. Hollenbeck began the process of putting him at his ease. There was no need. The tutor was quite as much at ease as any one, and, in a little while, imperceptibly became the person to whom we were all listening.

Charlotte Benson at last gave up her book, and took her work-box instead. We were no longer moping and dull around the table. And bye and bye Henrietta, much alarmed, was sent to the piano, and her poor little music certainly sounded very meagre when Mr. Langenau touched the keys.

I think he consented to play not to appear rude,

but with the firm intention of not being the instrument of our entertainment, and not being made use of out of his own accepted calling. But happily for us, he soon forgot all about us, and played on, absorbed in himself and in his music. We listened breathlessly, the others quite as much engrossed as I, because they all knew much more of music than I did. Suddenly, after playing for a long while, he started from the piano, and came back to the table. He was evidently agitated. Before the others could say a word of thanks or wonder, I cried, in a fear of the cessation of what gave me such intense pleasure,

" Oh, sing something; can't you sing ?"

" Yes, I can sing," he said, looking down at me with those dangerous eyes. " Will it give you pleasure if I sing for you ?"

He did not wait for an answer, but turned back to the piano.

He had said " if I sing for you," and I knew that for me he was singing. I do not know what it was for others, but for me, it was the only true music that I had ever heard, the only music that I could have begged might never cease, but flood over all the present and the future, satisfying every sense. Other voices had roused and thrilled, this filled me. I asked no more, and could have died with that sound in my ears.

"Why, Pauline! child! what is it?" cried Mrs. Hollenbeck, as the music ceased and Mr. Langenau again came back to the circle round the table. Every one looked: I was choking with sobs.

"Oh, don't, I don't want you to speak to me," I cried, putting away her hand and darting from the room. I was not ashamed of myself, even when I was alone in my room. The powerful magic lasted still, through the silence and darkness, till I was aroused by the voices of the others coming up to bed.

Mrs. Hollenbeck knocked at my door with her bedroom candle in her hand, and, as she stood talking to me, the others strayed in to join her and to satisfy their curiosity.

"You are very sensitive to music, are you not?" said Charlotte Benson, contemplatively. She had tried me on Mompsson, and the "Seven Lamps," and found me wanting, and now perhaps hoped to find some other point less faulty.

"I do not know," I said, honestly. "I seem to have been very sensitive to-night."

"But you are not always?" asked Henrietta Palmer. "You do not always cry when people sing?"

"Why, no," I said with great contempt. "But I never heard any one sing like that before."

"He does sing well," said Mrs. Hollenbeck, thoughtfully.

"Immense expression and a fine voice," added Charlotte Benson.

"He has been educated for the stage, you may be sure," said Mary Leighton, with a little spite. "As Miss d'Estrée says, I never heard any one sing like that, out of the chorus of an opera."

"Well, I think," returned Charlotte Benson, "if there were many voices like that in ordinary choruses, one would be glad to dispense with the solos and duets."

"Oh, you would not find his voice so wonderful, if you heard it out of a parlor. It is very well, but it would not fill a concert hall, much less an opera house. No; you may be sure he has been educated for some of those German choruses; you know they are very fine musicians."

"Well, I don't know that it is anything to us what he was educated for," said Charlotte Benson, sharply. "He has given us a very delightful evening, and I, for one, am much obliged to him."

"*Et moi aussi,*" murmured Henrietta, wreathing her large beautiful arms about her friend, and the two sauntered away.

Mary Leighton, in general ill-humor, and still remembering the walk of the last evening, desired to fire a parting-shot, and exclaimed, as she went out,

"Well, I think it is something to us; I like to have gentlemen about me."

"You need not be uneasy," said Mrs. Hollenbeck, a little stiffly. "I think Mr. Langenau is a gentleman."

But at this moment his step was heard in the hall below, and there was an end put to the conversation.

3*

CHAPTER VI.

MATINAL.

Last night, when some one spoke his name,
From my swift blood that went and came
A thousand little shafts of flame
Were shivered in my narrow frame.

Tennyson.

THE next morning was brilliant and cool, the earth and heavens shining after the rain of the past night. I was dressed long, long before breakfast: it would be so tiresome to wait in my room till the bell rang; yet if I went down-stairs, would it not look as if I wanted to see Mr. Langenau again? I need not go to the library, of course, but I could scarcely avoid being seen from the library if I went out. But why suppose that he would be down again so early? It was very improbable, and so, affectionately deceived, I put on a hat and walking-jacket and stole down the stairs. I saw by the clock in the lower hall that it was half an hour earlier than I had come down the morning before; at which I was secretly chagrined, for now there was no danger, *alias* hope, of seeing Mr. Langenau.

But probably he had forgotten all about the foolish half-hour that had given me so much to think about. I glanced into the library, which was empty, and hurried out of the hall-door, secretly disappointed.

I took the path that led over the hill to the river. It passed through the garden, under the long arbors of grapevines, over the hill, and through a grove of maples, ending at the river where the boat-house stood. The brightness of the morning was not lost on me, and before I reached the maple-grove I was buoyant and happy. At the entrance of the grove (which was traversed by several paths, the principal coming up directly from the river) I came suddenly upon the tutor, walking rapidly, with a pair of oars over his shoulder. He started, and for a moment we both stood still and did not speak. I could only think with confusion of my emotion when he sang.

"You are always early," he said, with his slight, very slight, foreign accent, "earlier than yesterday by half an hour," he added, looking at his watch. My heart gave a great bound of pleasure. Then he had not forgotten! How he must have seen all this.

He stood and talked with me for some moments, and then desperately I made a movement to go on. I do not believe, at least I am not sure, that at first he had any intention of going with me. But it was not

in human nature to withstand the flattery of such
emotion as his presence seemed always to inspire in
me; and then, I have no doubt, he had a certain
pleasure in talking to me outside of that; and then
the morning was so lovely and he had so much of
books.

He proposed to show me a walk I had not taken.
There was a little hesitation in his manner, but he
was reassured by my look of pleasure, and throwing
down the oars under a tree, he turned and walked beside me. No doubt he said to himself, "America!
This paradise of girlhood;—there can be no objection." It was heavenly sweet, that walk—the birds,
the sky, the dewiness and freshness of all nature and
all life. It seemed the unstained beginning of all
things to me.

The woods were wet; we could not go through
them, and so we went a longer way, along the river
and back by the road.

This time he did not do all the talking, but made
me talk, and listened carefully to all I said; and I was
so happy, talking was not any effort.

At last he made some allusion to the music of last
night; that he was so glad to see that I loved music as
I did. "But I don't particularly," I said in confusion,
with a great fear of being dishonest, "at least I never

thought I did before, and I am so ignorant. I don't want you to think I know anything about it, for you would be disappointed." He was silent, and, I felt sure, because he was already disappointed; in fear of which I went on to say—

"I never heard any one sing like that before; I am very sorry that it gave any one an impression that I had a knowledge of music, when I hadn't. I don't care about it generally, except in church, and I can't understand what made me feel so yesterday."

"Perhaps it is because you were in the mood for it," he said. "It is often so, one time music gives us pleasure, another time it does not."

"That may be so; but your voice, in speaking, even, seems to me different from any other. It is almost as good as music when you speak; only the music fills me with such feelings."

"You must let me sing for you again," he said, rather low, as we walked slowly on.

"Ah; if you only will," I answered, with a deep sigh of satisfaction.

We walked on in silence till we reached the gate: he opened it for me and then said, "Now I must leave you, and go back for the oars."

I was secretly glad of this; since the walk had reached its natural limit and its end must be accepted, it was a relief to approach the house alone and not be the subject of any observation.

Breakfast had began : no one seemed to feel much interest in my entrance, though flaming with red roses and red cheeks.

They were of the sex that do not notice such things naturally, with much interest or admiration. They had hardly "shaken off drowsy-hed," and had no pleasure in anything but their breakfast, and not much in that.

"How do you manage to get yourself up and dressed at such inhuman hours?" said Mary Leighton, querulously.

"You are a reproach to the household, and we will not suffer it," said Charlotte Benson.

"I never could understand this thing of getting up before you are obliged to," added Henrietta plaintively.

But Sophie seemed well satisfied, particularly when Mr. Langenau came in and I looked down into my cup of tea, instead of saying good-morning to him. He did not say very much, though there was a good deal of babble among the others, principally.about his music.

It was becoming the fashion to be very attentive to him. He was made to promise to play in the evening; to bring down his books of music for the benefit of Miss Henrietta, who wanted to practice, Heaven knows what of his. His advice was asked about styles of playing and modes of instruction; he was deferred to as an authority. But very little he seemed to care about it all, I thought.

CHAPTER VII.

Qui va à la chasse perd sa place.

De la main à la bouche se perd souvent la soupe.

> Distance all value enhances !
> When a man's busy, why, leisure
> Strikes him as wonderful pleasure.
> Faith ! and at leisure once is he,
> Straightway he wants to be busy.
> *R. Browning.*

Two weeks more passed : two weeks that seem to me so many years when I look back upon them. Many more walks, early and late, many evenings of music, many accidents of meeting. It is all like a dream. At seventeen it is so easy to dream! It does not take two weeks for a girl to fall in love and make her whole life different.

It was Saturday evening, and Richard was expected; Richard and Kilian and Mr. Eugene Whitney. Ah, Richard was coming just three weeks too late.

We were all waiting on the piazza for them, in pretty toilettes and excellent tempers. It was a lovely evening; the sunset was filling the sky with splendor, and Charlotte and Henrietta had gone to the corner of the piazza whence the river could be seen, and were murmuring fragments of verses to each other. They were not so much absorbed, however, but that they heard the first sound of the wheels inside the gate, and hurried back to join us by the steps.

Mary Leighton looked absolutely lovely. The blue organdie had seen the day at last, and she was in such a flutter of delight at the coming of the gentlemen that she could scarcely be recognized as the pale, flimsy young person who had moped so unblushingly all the week.

" They are all three there," she exclaimed with suppressed rapture, as the carriage turned the angle of the road that brought them into sight. Mrs. Hollenbeck, quite beaming with pleasure, ran down the steps (for Richard had been away almost two months), and Mary Leighton was at her side, of course. Charlotte Benson and Henrietta went half-way down the steps, and I stood on the piazza by the pillar near the door. .

I was a little excited by their coming, too, but not nearly as much so as I might have been three weeks ago. A subject of much greater interest occupied my mind that very moment, and related to the chances of the tutor's getting home in time for tea, from one

of those long walks that were so tiresome. I felt as
if I hardly needed Richard now. Still, dear old Richard! It was very nice to see him once again.

The gentlemen all sprang out of the carriage, and
a Babel of welcomes and questions and exclamations
arose. Richard kissed his sister, and answered some
of her many questions, then shook hands with the
young ladies, but I could see that his eye was search-
ing for me. I can't tell why, certainly not because I
felt at all shy, I had stepped back, a little behind the
pillar and the vines. In an instant he saw me, and
came quickly up the steps, and stood by me and
grasped my hand, and looked exactly as if he meant
to kiss me. I hoped that nobody saw his look, and I
drew back, a little frightened. Of course, I know
that he had not the least intention of kissing me, but
his look was so eager and so unusual.

"It is two months, Pauline," he said; "and are you
well?" And though I only said that I was well and
was very glad to see him, I am sure his sister Sophie
thought that it was something more, for she had followed him up the steps and stood in the doorway
looking at us.

The others came up there, and Kilian, as soon as
he could get out of the meshes of the blue organdie,
came to me, and tried to out-devotion Richard.

That is the way with men. He had not taken any trouble to get away from Mary Leighton till Richard came.

A young woman only needs one lover very much in earnest, to bring about her several others, not so much, perhaps, in earnest, but very amusing and instructive. Richard went away very quickly, for I am sure he did not like that sort of thing.

It was soon necessary for Mr. Kilian to suspend his devotion and go to his room to get ready for tea.

When we all assembled again, at the table, I found that he had placed himself beside me, next his sister, little Benny having gone to bed.

" Of course, the head of the table belongs to Richard; I never interfere there, and as everybody else is placed, this is the only seat that I can take, following the rose and thorn principle."

" But that principle is not followed strictly," cried Charlotte Benson, who sat by Mary Leighton. " Here are two roses and no thorn."

" Ah! What a strange oversight," he exclaimed, seating himself nevertheless. " The only way to remedy it will be to put the tutor in your place, Miss Benson, and you come opposite Miss Pauline. Quick; before he comes and refuses to move his Teutonic bones an inch." Charlotte Benson changed her

seat and the vacant one was left between her and
Mary Leighton.

This is the order of our seats, for that and many
following happy nights and days:

Richard,

Mary Leighton,	Henrietta,
The Tutor,	Mr. Eugene Whitney,
Charlotte Benson,	Myself,
Charley,	Kilian,

Sophie.   •

Mary Leighton looked furious and could hardly
speak a word all through the meal. It was particularly hard upon her, as the tutor did not come, and
the chair was empty, and a glaring insult to her all
the time.

Kilian had done his part so innocently and so
simply that it was hard to suspect him of any
intention to pique her and annoy Richard, but I am
sure he did it with just those two intentions. He was
as thorough a flirt as any woman, and withal very
fond of change, and I think my pink grenadine quite
dazzled him as I stood on the piazza. Then came the
brotherly and quite natural desire to outshine Richard
and put things out a little. I liked it all very much,
and was charmed to be of so much consequence, for I
saw all this quite plainly. I laughed and talked a

good deal with Kilian ; he was delightful to laugh and talk with. Even Eugene Whitney found me more worth his weak attention than the beautiful and placid Henrietta.

The amusement was chiefly at our end of the table. But amidst it, I did not fail to glance often at the door and wonder, uncomfortably, why the tutor did not come.

As we left the table and lingered for a few moments in the hall, Richard came up to me and said, as he prepared to light his cigar, "Will you not come out and walk up and down the path here with me while I smoke ?"

I began to make some excuse, for I wanted to do nothing just then but watch the stairway to see if Mr. Langenau did not come down even then and go into the dining-room.

But I reflected how ungracious it would seem to refuse this, when he had just come home, and I followed him out into the path.

There was no moon, but the stars were very bright, and the air was sweet with the flower-beds in the grass along the path we walked.

The house looked gay and pleasant as we walked up and down before it, with its many lighted windows, and people with bright dresses moving about on the piazza. Richard lit his cigar, and said, after a silence of a few moments, with a sigh, "It is good to be at home again."

"But you've had a pleasant journey?"

"No; the most tiresome that I ever made, and this last detention wore my patience out. It seemed the longest fortnight. I could not bear to think of you all here, and I away in such a dismal hole."

"I suppose Uncle Leonard had no pity on you, as long as there was a penny to be made by staying there."

"No; I spent a great deal of money in telegraphing to him for orders to come home, but he would not give up."

"And how is Uncle Leonard; did you go to Varick-street?"

"No, indeed; I did not waste any time in town. I only reached there yesterday."

"I wonder Uncle Leonard let you off so soon."

"He growled a good deal, but I did not stay to listen."

"That's always the best way."

"And now, Pauline, tell me how you like the place."

"Like it! Oh, Richard, I think it is a Paradise," and I clasped my hands in a young sort of ecstacy.

He was silent, which was a sign that he was satisfied

I went on after a moment, "I don't wonder that you all love it. I never saw anything half so beautiful. The dear old house is prettier than any new one that could be built, and the trees are so grand! And oh, Richard, I think the garden lying on the hillside there in the beautiful warm sun, with such royal flowers and fruit, is worth all the grape-houses and conservatories in the neighborhood. Your sister took us to three or four of the neighboring places a week or two ago. But I like this a hundred times the best. I should think you would be sorry every moment that you have to spend away from it."

"I hope one of these days to live here altogether," he said in a low tone.

It was so difficult for Richard to be unreserved that it is very likely this was the first time in his life that he had ever expressed this, the brightest hope he had.

I could fancy all these few words implied— a wife, children, a happy home in manhood where he had been a happy child.

"It belongs to Kilian and me, but it is understood I have the right to it when I am ready for it."

"And your sister—it does not belong at all to her?"

"No, she only keeps house for us. It would make a great change for Sophie if either of us married.

But then I know that it would give her pleasure, for
I am sure that she would not be selfish."

I was not so sure, but, of course, I did not say so.
At this moment, while Richard smoked and I walked
silently beside him, a dark figure struck directly
across the path before us. The apparition was so
sudden that I sprang and screamed, and caught
Richard by the arm.

"I beg your pardon," said the tutor, with a quick
look of surprise at me and then at Richard, and bow-
ing, strode on into the house.

"That's the German Sophie has taken for the boys,
is it?" said Richard, knitting his brows, and looking
after him, with no great approbation. "I don't half
like the idea of his being here: I told Sophie so at
starting. A governess would do as well for two years
yet. What kind of a person does he seem to be?"

"I don't know—that is—I can't tell exactly. I
don't know him well enough," I answered in confusion, which Richard did not see.

"No, of course not. You would not be likely to
see him except at the table. But it is awkward having him here,—so much of the week, no man about;
and one never knows anything about these Germans."

"I thought—your sister said—you knew all about
him," I said, in rather a low voice.

"As much as one needs to know about a mere teacher. But the person you have in your house all the time is different."

"But he is a gentleman," I put in more firmly.

"I hope he is. He had letters to some friends of ours. But what are letters? People give them when they're asked for them, and half the time know nothing of the person for whom they do the favor, besides his name and general standing. Hardly that, sometimes." Then, as if to put away a tiresome and unwelcome subject, he began again to talk about the place.

But I had lost my interest in the subject, and thought only of returning to the house.

"Don't," I said, playfully putting out my hand as he took out another cigar to light. "You have smoked enough to-night. Do you know, you smoke a great deal more than is good for you."

"Well, I will not smoke any more to-night if you say so. Only don't go in the house."

"Oh, yes, you know we only came out to smoke."

He stood in front of the path that led to the piazza and said, in an affectionate, gentle way, "Stay and walk a little longer. I have not told you half how glad I am that you are here at last."

"Oh, as for that, you've got a good many weeks to

4

tell me in. Besides, it's getting chilly," and I gave a little shiver.

"If you're cold, of course," he said, letting me pass and following me, and added, with a shade of anxiety, "Why didn't you tell me before? I never thought of it, and you have no shawl."

I felt ashamed of myself as I led the way up the piazza steps.

In the hall, which was quite light, they were all standing, and Mr. Langenau was in the group. They were petitioning him for music.

"Oh, he has promised that he will sing," said Sophie; "but remember he has not had his tea. I have ordered it for you, Mr. Langenau; it will be ready in a moment."

Mr. Langenau bowed and turned to go up the stairs. His eye met mine, as I came into the light, dazzled a little by it.

He went up the stairs; the others after a few moments, went into the parlor. I sat down on a sofa beside Mrs. Hollenbeck. Richard was called away by a person on business. There was a shaded lamp on a bracket above the sofa where we sat; Mrs. Hollenbeck was reading some letters she had just received, and I took up the evening paper, reading over and over an advertisement of books. Presently the servant came

to Mrs. Hollenbeck and said that Mr. Langenau's tea
was ready. She was sent up to tell him so, and in a
few moments he came down. When he reached the
hall, Sophie looked up with her most lovely smile.

"You must be famished, Mr. Langenau; pray go
immediately to the dining-room. I am sorry not to
make your tea myself, but I hear Benny waking and
must go to him. Will you mind taking my place,
Pauline, and pouring out tea for Mr. Langenau?"

I was bending over the paper; my face turned
suddenly from red to pale. I said something
inaudible in reply, and got up and went into the
dining-room, followed by the tutor.

It was several minutes before I looked at him. The
servants had not favored us with much light: there
was a branch of wax candles in the middle of the
table. Mr. Langenau's plate was placed just at one
side of the tray, at which I had seated myself. He
looked pale, even to his lips. I began to think of the
terrible walks in which he seemed to hunt himself
down, and to wonder what was the motive, though I
had often wondered that before. He took the cup of
tea I offered him without speaking. Neither of us
spoke for several minutes, then I said, rather irreso-
lutely, "I am sure you tire yourself by these long
walks."

"Do you think so? No: they rest me."

No doubt I felt more coquettish, and had more con-fidence than usual, from the successes of that evening, and from the knowledge that Richard and Kilían and Eugene Whitney, even, were so delighted to talk to me; otherwise I could never have said what I said then, by a sudden impulse, and with a half-laughing voice, "Do not go away again so long; it makes it so dull and tiresome."

He looked at me and said, "It does not seem to me you miss me very much." But such a gleam of those dark, dangerous eyes! I looked down, but my breath came quickly and my face must have shown the agita-tion that I felt.

At this moment Richard, released from his engage-ment in the library, came through the hall and stopped at the dining-room door. He paused for a moment at the door, walked away again, then came back and into the room, with rather a quicker step than usual.

"Pauline," he said, and I started visibly, "They seem to be waiting for you in the parlor for a game of cards."

His voice indicated anything but satisfaction. I half rose, then sank back, and said, hesitatingly, "Can I pour you some more tea, Mr. Langenau?"

"If it is not troubling you too much," he said in a

voice that a moment's time had hardened into sharpness.

Oh, the misery of that cup of tea, with Richard looking at me on one side flushed and angry, and Mr. Langenau on the other, pale and cynical. My hands shook so that I could not lift the tea-kettle, and Richard angrily leaned down and moved it for me. The alcohol in the lamp flamed up and scorched my arm.

"Oh Richard, you have burned me," I cried, dropping the cup and wrapping my handkerchief around my arm. In an instant he was all softness and kindness, and, I have no doubt, repentance.

"I am very sorry," he said; "Does it hurt you very much? Come with me, and I will get Sophie to put something on it."

But Mr. Langenau did not move or show any interest in my sufferings. I was half-crying, but I sat still and tried with the other hand to replace the cup and fill it. Seeing that I did not make much headway, and that Richard had stepped back, Mr. Langenau said, "Allow me," and held the cup while I managed to pour the tea into it. He thanked me stiffly, and without looking at either of them I got up and went out of the room, Richard following me.

"Will you wait here while I call Sophie to get something for you?" he said a little coldly.

"No, I do not want anything; I wish you would not say anything more about it; it only hurt me for a moment."

"Will you go into the parlor, then?"

"No—yes, that is," I said, and capriciously went, alone, for he did not follow me.

I was wanted for cards, but I would not play, and sat down by one of the windows, a little out of the light. This window opened upon the piazza. After a little while Richard, walking up and down the piazza, stopped by it, and said to me: "I hope you won't think it unreasonable in me to ask, Pauline; but how in the world did you happen to be making tea for that—that man in there?"

"I happened to make tea for Mr. Langenau because your sister asked me to," I said angrily; "you had better speak to her about it."

"You may be sure I shall," he said, walking away from the window.

Presently the tutor came in from the hall by the door near the piano, and sat down by it without being asked, and began to play softly, as if not to interrupt the game of cards. I could not help thinking in what good taste this was, since he had promised not to wait for any more importunities. The game at cards soon languished, for Charlotte Benson really had an enthusiasm for music, and was not happy till she was at liberty to give her whole attention to it. As soon as the players were released, Kilian came over and sat beside me. He rather wearied me, for I wanted to listen to the music, but he was determined not to see that, and chattered so that more than once Charlotte Benson turned impatiently and begged us not to talk. Once Mr. Langenau himself turned and looked at us, but Kilian only paused, and then went on again.

Mary Leighton had fled to the piano and was gazing at the keys in a rapt manner, hoping, no doubt, to rouse Kilian to jealousy of the tutor.

"Please go away," I said at last, "this is making me seem rude."

"Do not tell me," he exclaimed, "that you are helping Mary Leighton and Sophie to spoil this German fellow. I really did not look for it in you. I—"

"I can't stay here and be talked to," I said, getting up in despair.

"Then come on the piazza," he exclaimed, and we were there almost before I knew what I was doing.

I suppose every one in the room saw us go out: I was in terror when I thought what an insult it would seem to Mr. Langenau. We walked about the piazza for some time; I am afraid Mr. Kilian found me

rather dull, for I could only listen to what was going
on inside. At last he was called away by a man from
the stable, who brought some alarming account of his
·beloved Tom or Jerry. If I had been his bride at
the altar, I am sure he would have left me; being
only a new and very faintly-lighted flame, he hurried
off with scarcely an apology.

I sat down in a piazza-chair, just outside the window at which we had been sitting. I looked in at the
window, but no one could see me, from the position
of my chair.

Presently Mr. Langenau left the piano, and Mary
Leighton, talking to him with effusion, walked across
the room beside him, and took her seat at this very
window. He did not sit down, but stood before her
with his hat in his hand, as if he only awaited a favorable pause to go away.

"Ah, where did Pauline go?" she said, glancing
around. "But I suppose we must excuse her, for to-
night at least, as he has just come home. I imagine
the engagement was no surprise to you?"

"Of what engagement do you speak?" he said.

"Why! Pauline and Richard Vandermarck; you
know it is quite a settled thing. And very good for
her, I think. He seems to me just the sort of man to
keep her steady and—well, improve her character, you

know. She seems such a heedless sort of girl. They say her mother ran away and made some horrid marriage, and, I believe, her uncle has had to keep her very strict. He is very much pleased, I am told, with marrying her to Richard, and she herself seems very much in love with him."

All this time he had stood very still and looked at her, but his face had changed slowly as she spoke. I knew then that what she had said had not pleased him. She went on in her babbling, soft voice:

" His sister Sophie isn't pleased, of course, so there is nothing said about it here. It *is* rather hard for her, for the place belongs to Richard, and besides, Richard has been very generous to her always. And then to see him marry just such a sort of person—you know—so young—"

" Yes—so young," said Mr. Langenau, between his teeth, "and of such charming innocence."

" Oh, as to that," said Mary Leighton, piqued beyond prudence, " we all have our own views as to that."

The largess due the bearer of good news was not by right the meed of Mary Leighton. He looked at her as if he hated her.

" Mr. Richard Vandermarck is a fortunate man," he said. " She has rare beauty, if he has a taste for beauty."

4*

"Men sometimes tire of that; if indeed she has it. Her coloring is her strong point, and that may not last forever;" and Mary's voice was no longer silvery.

"You think so?" he said. "I think her grace is her strong point, '*la grâce encore plus belle que la beauté,*' and longer-lived beside. Few women move as she does, making it a pleasure to follow her with the eyes. And her height and suppleness: at twenty-five she will be regal."

"Then, Mr. Langenau," she cried, with sudden spitefulness, "you *do* admire her very much yourself! Do you know, I thought perhaps you did. How you must envy Mr. Vandermarck!"

A slight shrug of the shoulders and a slight low laugh; after which, he said, "No, I think not. I have not the courage that is necessary."

"The courage! why, what do you mean by that?"

"I mean that a man who ventures to love a woman in whom he cannot trust, has need for courage and for patience; perhaps Mr. Richard Vandermarck has them both abundantly. For me, I think the pretty Miss Pauline would be safer as an hour's amusement than as a life's companion."

The words stabbed, killed me. With an ejaculation that could scarcely have escaped their ears, I sprang up and ran through the hall and up the stairs. Be-

fore I reached the landing-place, I knew that some
one was behind me. I did not look or pause, but flew
on through the hall till I reached my own door. My
own door was just at the foot of the third-floor stairway. I glanced back, and saw that it was Mr. Langenau who was behind me. I pushed open my door and
went half-way in the room; then with a vehement
and sudden impulse came back into the hall and
pulled it shut again and stood with my hand upon the
latch, and waited for him to pass. In an instant more
he was near me, but not as if he saw me; he could
not reach the stairway without passing so near me
that he must touch my dress. I waited till he was so
near, and said, " Mr. Langenau."

He raised his eyes steadily to mine and bowed low.
I almost choked for one instant, and then I found
voice and rushed on vehemently. "What she has told
you is false ; every word of it is false. I am not engaged
to Richard Vandermarck ; I never thought of such
a thing till I came here, and found they talked about
t. They ought to be ashamed, and I will go away
to-morrow. And what she said about my mother is a
wicked lie as well, at least in the way she meant it ;
and I shall hate her all my life. I have been mother-
less and lonely always, but God has cared for me, and
I never knew before what evil thoughts and ways there

were. I am not ashamed that I listened, though I didn't mean to stay at first. I'm glad I heard it all and know what kind of friends I have. And those last cruel words you said—I never will forgive you, never—never—never till I die."

He had put his hand out toward me as if in conciliation, at least I understood it so. I pushed it passionately away, rushed into my room, bolted the door, and flung myself upon the bed with a frightful burst of sobs. I heard his hand upon the latch of the door, and he said my name several times in a low voice. Then he went slowly up the stairs. And I think his room must have been directly over mine, for, for hours I heard some one walking there; indeed, it was the last sound I heard, when, having cried all my tears and vowed all my vows, I fell asleep and forgot that I was wretched.

CHAPTER VIII.

La notte é madre di pensieri.

Now tell me how you are as to religion ?
You are a dear good man—but I rather fear
You have not much of it.

Faust.   .

IT was all very well to talk about going away ; but
the matter looked very differently by daylight. It
was Sunday ; and I knew I could not go away for a
day or two, and not even then without making a
horrid sort of stir, for which I had not the courage in
cold blood.   Besides, I did not even know ' that I
wanted to go if I could.   Varick-street!   Hateful,
hateful thought.   No, I could not go there.   And
though (by daylight) I still detested Mary Leighton,
and felt ashamed about Richard, and remembered all
Mr. Langenau's words (sweet as well as bitter), everything was let down a great many degrees ; from the
heights of passion into the plains of commonplace.

My great excitement had worked its own cure, and
I was so dull and weary that I did not even want to
think of what had passed the night before.   If I had

a sentiment that retained any strength, it was that of shame and self-contempt. I could not think of myself in any way that did not make me blush. When, however, it came to the moment of facing every one, and going down to breakfast, I began to know I still had some other feelings.

I was the last to go down. The bell had rung a very long while before I left my room. I took my seat at the table without looking at any one, though, of course, every one looked at me. My confused and rather general good-morning was returned with much precision by all. Somebody remarked that I did not look well. Somebody else remarked that was surely because I went to bed so early; that it never had been known to agree with any one. Some one else wanted to know why I had gone so early, and that I had been hunted for in all directions for a dance which had been a sudden inspiration.

"But as you had gone away, and the musician could not be found, we had to give it up," said Charlotte Benson, "and we owe you both a grudge."

"For my part, I am very sorry," said Mr. Langenau. "I had no thought that you meant to dance last night, or I should have stayed at the piano; I hope you will tell me the next time."

"The next time will be to-morrow evening," said

Mary Leighton. "Now, Mr. Langenau, you will not forget—or—or get excited about anything and go away?"

I dared not look at Mr. Langenau's face, but I am sure I should not have seen anything pleasant if I had. I don't know what he answered, for I was so confused, I dropped a plate of berries which I was just taking from Kilian's hand, and made quite an uncomfortable commotion. The berries were very ripe, and they rolled in many directions on the table-cloth, and fell on my white dress.

"Your pretty dress is ruined, I'm afraid," said Kilian, stooping down to save it.

"I don't care about that, but I'm very sorry that I've stained the table-cloth," and I looked at Mrs. Hollenbeck as if I thought that she would scold me for it. But she quite reassured me. Indeed, I think she was so pleased with me, that she would not have minded seeing me ruin all the table-cloths that she had.

"But it will make you late for church, for you'll have to change your dress," said Charlotte Benson, practically, glancing at the clock. I was very thankful for the suggestion, for I thought it would save me from the misery of trying to eat breakfast, but Kilian made such an outcry that I found I could not go without more comments than I liked.

" You have no appetite either," said Mary Leighton. "I am ashamed to eat as much as I want, for here is Mr. Langenau beside me, who has only broken a roll in two and drank a cup of coffee."

"I am not perhaps quite used to your American way of breakfasting," he returned quickly.

" But you ate breakfasts when we first came," said the sweet girl gently.

" Was not the weather cooler then?" he answered, "and I have missed my walk this morning."

"Let me give you some more coffee, at any rate," said Sophie, with affectionate interest. Indeed, I think at that moment she absolutely loved him.

In a few minutes I escaped from the table; when I came down from my room ready for church, I found that they were all just starting. (Richard, I suppose, would have waited for me.) The church was in the village, and not ten minutes' walk from the house. Kilian was carrying Mary Leighton's prayer-book, and was evidently intending to walk with her.

Richard came up to me and said, " Sophie is waiting to know if you will let her drive you, or if you will walk."

I had not yet been obliged to speak to Richard since I had heard what people said about us, and I felt uncomfortable.

"Oh, let me drive if there is room," I said, without looking up. Sophie sat in her little carriage waiting for me. Richard put me in beside her, and then joined the others, while we drove away. Benny, in his white Sunday clothes, sat at our feet.

"I think it is so much better for you to drive," said Mrs. Hollenbeck, "for the day is warm, and I did not think you looked at all well this morning."

"No," I said faintly. And she was so kind, I longed to tell her everything. It is frightful at seventeen to have no one to tell your troubles to.

At the gate Benny was just grumbling about getting out to open it, when Mr. Langenau appeared, and held it open for us. He was dressed in a flannel suit which he wore for walking. After he closed the gate, he came up beside the carriage, as Mrs. Hollenbeck very kindly invited him to do, by driving slowly.

"Are you coming with us to church, Mr. Langenau?" asked Benny.

"To church? No, Benny. I am afraid they would not let me in."

"Why, yes, they would, if you had your good clothes on," said Benny.

Mr. Langenau laughed, a little bitterly, and said he doubted, even then. "I am afraid I haven't got my good conscience on either, Benny."

"But the minister would never know," said Benny.

"That's very true; the ministers here don't know much about peoples' consciences, I should think."

"Do ministers in any other places know any more?" asked Benny with interest.

"Why, yes, Benny, in a good many countries where I've been, they do."

"You are a Catholic, Mr. Langenau?" asked Mrs. Hollenbeck.

"I once was; I have no longer any right to say it is my faith," he answered slowly.

"What is it to be a Catholic?" inquired Benny, gazing at his tutor's face with wonder.

"To be a Catholic, is to be in a safe prison; to have been a Catholic, is to be alone on a sea big and black with billows, Benny."

"I think I'd like the prison best," said Benny, who was very much afraid of the water.

"Ah, but if you couldn't get back to it, my boy."

"Well, I think I'd try to get to land somewhere," Benny answered, stoutly.

Mr. Langenau laughed, but rather gloomily, and we went on for a few moments in silence. The road was bordered with trees, and there was a beautiful shade. The horse was very glad to be permitted to go slow, not being of an ambitious nature.

All this time I had been leaning back, holding my parasol very close over my face. Mr. Langenau happened to be on the side by me: once when the carriage had leaned suddenly, he had put his hand upon it, and had touched, without intending it, my arm.

"I beg your pardon," he had said, and that was all he had said to me; and I had felt very grateful that Benny had been so inclined to talk. I trusted that nobody would speak to me, for my voice would never be steady and even again, I was sure, when he was by to listen to it.

Now, however, he spoke to me: commonplace words, the same almost that every one in the house had addressed to me that morning, but how differently they sounded.

"I am sorry that you are not well to-day, Miss d'Estrée."

Mrs. Hollenbeck at this moment began to find some fault with Benny's gloves, and leaning down, talked very obligingly and earnestly with him, while she fastened the gloves upon his hands.

Mr. Langenau took the occasion, as it was intended he should take it, and said rather low, "You will not refuse to see me a few moments this evening, that I may explain something to you?"

I think he was disappointed that I did not answer

him, only turned away my head.   But I don't know
in truth what other answer he had any right to ask.
He did not attempt to speak again, but as we turned
into the village, said, " Good-morning, I must leave
you.   Good-bye, Benny, since I have neither clothes
nor conscience fit for church."

Sophie laughed, and said, at least she hoped he
would be home for dinner.   He did not promise, but
raising his hat struck off into a little path by the road-
side, that led up into the woods.

"What a pity," said Mrs. Hollenbeck musingly,
" that a man of such fine intellect should have such
vague religious faith."

Mr. Langenau was not home for dinner, but he did
not see me at that meal, for my head ached so, and I
felt so weary that when I came up-stairs after church,
it seemed impossible to go down again.   I should have
been very glad to make the same excuse serve for the
remainder of the day, but really the rest and a cup of
tea had so restored me, that no excuse remained at six
o'clock.

All families have their little Sunday habits, I have
found; the Sunday rule in this house was, to have tea
at half-past six, and to walk by the river till after the
sun had set; then to come home and have sacred
music in the parlor.   After tea, accordingly, we took

our shawls on our arms (it still being very warm) and walked down toward the river.

I kept beside Mrs. Hollenbeck and Benny, where only I felt safe.

The criticism I had heard had given me such a shock, I did not feel that I ever could be careful enough of what I said and did. And I vaguely felt my mother's honor would be vindicated, if I showed myself always a modest and prudent woman.

"It was so well that I heard them," I kept saying to myself, but I felt so much older and so much graver. My silence and constraint were no doubt differently interpreted. Richard did not come up to me, except to tell me I had better put my shawl on, as I sat on the steps of the boat-house, with Benny beside me. The others had walked further on and were sitting, some of them on the rocks, and some on the boat that had been drawn up, watching the sun go down.

"Tell me a story," said Benny, resting his arms on my lap, "a story about when you were a little girl."

"Oh, Benny, that wouldn't make a pretty story."

"Oh, yes, it would: all about your mamma and the house you used to live in, and the children you used to go to see."

"Dear Benny! I never lived in but one old, dismal

house. I never went to play with any children. I
could not make a story out of that."

" But your mamma. O yes, I'm sure you could if
you tried very hard."

"Ah, Benny! that's the worst of all. For my
mamma has been with God and the good angels in
the sky, ever since I was a little baby, and I have
had a dreary time without her here alone."

" Then I think you might tell me about God and
the good angels," whispered Benny, getting closer
to me.

I wrapped my arms around him, and leaning my
face down upon his yellow curls, told him a story of
God and the good angels in the sky.

Dear little Benny! I always loved him from that
night. He cried over my story : that I suppose wins
everybody's heart: and we went together, looking at
the placid river and the pale blue firmament, very far
into the paradise of faith. My tears dropped upon
his upturned face; and when the stars came out, and
we were told it was time to go back to the house,
we went back hand in hand, firm friends for all life
from that Sunday night.

· " There is Mr. Langenau," said Benny; "waiting
for you, I should think."

Mr. Langenau was waiting for me at the piazza

steps. He fixed his eyes on mine as if waiting for my permission to speak again. But I fastened my eyes upon the ground, and holding Benny tightly by the hand, went on into the house.

CHAPTER IX.

A DANCE.

It is impossible to love and to be wise.

Bacon.

Niente piu tosto se secca che lagrime.

"This is what we must do about it," said Kilian, as we sat around the breakfast-table. "If you are still in a humor for the dance to-night, I will order Tom and Jerry to be brought up at once, and Miss Pauline and I will go out and deliver all the invitations."

"Of which there are about five," said Charlotte Benson. "You can spare Tom and Jerry and send a small boy."

"But what if I had rather go myself?" he said, "and Miss Pauline needs the air. Now there are— let me see," and he began to count up the dancing inhabitants of the neighborhood.

"Will you write notes or shall we leave a verbal message at each door?"

"Oh leave a verbal message by all means," said Charlotte Benson, a little sharply. "It won't be quite *en règle,* as Miss d'Estrée doesn't know the people, but so unconventional and fresh."

"I do know them," I retorted, much annoyed, "conventionally at least: for they have all called upon me, though I didn't see them all. But I shall be very glad if you will take my place."

"Oh, thank you; I wasn't moving an amendment for that end. We have made our arrangements for the morning, irrespective of the delivery of cards."

"I shall have time to write the notes first, if Sophie would rather have notes sent," said Henrietta, who wrote a good hand and was very fond of writing people's notes for them.

"Oh, thank you, dear; yes, perhaps it would be best, and save Pauline and Kilian trouble."

So Henrietta went grandly away to write her little notes: a very large ship on a very small voyage.

"And how about your music, Sophie," said Kilian, who was anxious to have all business matters settled relating to the evening.

"Well, I suppose you had better go for the music-teacher from the village; he plays very well for dancing, and it is a mercy to me and to poor Henrietta, who would have to be pinned to the piano for the evening, if we didn't have him."

"As to that, I thought we had a music-teacher of

5

our own: can't your German be made of any practical account? Or is he only to be looked at and revered for his great powers?"

"I didn't engage Mr. Langenau to play for us to dance," said Sophie.

"Nor to lounge about the parlor every evening either," muttered Kilian, pushing away his cup of coffee.

"Now, Mr. Kilian, pray don't let our admiration of the tutor drive you into any bitterness of feeling," cried Charlotte Benson, who had been treasuring up a store of little slights from Kilian. "You know he can't be blamed for it, poor man."

Kilian was so much annoyed that he did not trust himself to answer, but rose from the table, and asked me if I would drive with him in half an hour.

During the drive, he exclaimed angrily that Charlotte Benson had a tongue that would drive a man to suicide if he came in hearing of it daily. "Why, if she were as beautiful as a goddess, I could never love her. Depend upon it, she'll never get a husband, Miss Pauline."

"Some men like to be scolded, I have heard," I said.

"Well then, if you ever stumble upon one that does, just call me and I'll run and fetch him Charlotte Benson."

The morning was lovely, and I had much pleasure in the drive, though I had not gone with any idea of enjoying it. It was very exhilarating to drive so fast as Kilian always drove; and Kilian himself always amused me and made me feel at ease. We were very companionable; and though I could not understand how young ladies could make a hero of him, and fancy that they loved him, I could quite understand how they should find him delightful and amusing.

We delivered our notes, at more than one place, into the hands of those to whom they were addressed, and had many pleasant talks at the piazza steps with young ladies whom I had not known before. Then we went to the village and engaged the music-teacher, stopped at the "store" and left some orders, and drove to the Post-Office to see if there were letters.

"Haven't we had a nice morning!" I exclaimed simply, as we drove up to the gate.

"Capital," said Kilian. "I'm afraid it's been the best part of the day. I wish I had any assurance that the German would be half as pleasant. I beg your pardon, I don't mean your surly Teuton, but the dance that we propose to-night; I wish it had another name. Confound it! there he is ahead of us. (I don't mean the dance this time, you see.) I wish he'd turn back and open the gate for us. Holloa there!"

Kilian would not have dared call out, if the boys had not been with their tutor. It was one o'clock, and they were coming from the farm-house back to dinner. At the call they all turned; Mr. Langenau stood still, and told Charles to go back and open the gate.

Kilian frowned; he didn't like to see his nephew ordered to do anything by this unpleasant German. While we were waiting for the opening of the gate, the tutor walked on toward the house with Benny. As we passed them, Benny called out, "Stop, Uncle Kilian, stop, and take me in." Benny never was denied anything, so we stopped and Mr. Langenau lifted him up in front of us. He bowed without speaking, and Benny was the orator of the occasion.

"You looked as if you were having such a nice time, I thought I'd like to come."

"Well, we were," said Kilian, with a laugh, and then we drove on rapidly.

At the tea-table Mr. Langenau said to Sophie as he rose to go away: "Mrs. Hollenbeck, if there is any service I can render you this evening at the piano, I shall be very glad if you will let me know."

Mrs. Hollenbeck thanked him with cordiality, but told him of the provision that had been made.

"But you will dance, Mr. Langenau," cried Mary Leighton, "we need dancing-men terribly, you know. Promise me you'll dance."

"Oh," said Charlotte Benson, "he has promised me." Mr. Langenau bowed low; he got wonderfully through these awkward situations. As he left the room Kilian said in a tone loud enough for us, but not for him, to hear, "The Lowders have a nice young gardener; hadn't we better send to see if he can't come this evening?"

"Kilian, that's going a little too far," said Richard in a displeased manner; "as long as the boys' tutor conducts himself like a gentleman, he deserves to be treated like a gentleman."

"Ah, Paterfamilias, thank you. Yes, I'll think of it," and Kilian proposed that we should leave the table, as we all seemed to have appeased our appetites and nothing but civil war could come of staying any longer.

It was understood we had not much time to dress: but when I came down-stairs, none of the others had appeared. Richard met me in the hall: he had been rather stern to me all day, but his manner quite softened as he stood beside me under the hall-lamp.

That was the result of my lovely white mull, with its mint of Valenciennes.

"You haven't any flowers," he said.   Heavens! who'd have thought he'd ever have spoken in such a tone again, after the cup of tea I poured out for the tutor.   "Let's go and see if we can't find some in these vases that are fit, for I suppose the garden's robbed."

"Yes," I said, following him, quite pleased.   For I could not bear to have him angry with me.   I was really fond of him, dear, old Richard; and I looked so happy that I have no doubt he thought more of it than he ought.   He pulled all the pretty vases in the parlor to pieces: (Charlotte and Henrietta and his sister had arranged them with such care!) and made me a bouquet of ferns, and tea-roses, and lovely, lovely heliotrope.   I begged him to stop, but he went on till the flowers were all arranged and tied together, and no one came down-stairs till the spoilage was complete.

All this time Mr. Langenau was in the library—restless, pretending to read a book.   I saw him as we passed the door, but did not look again.   Presently we heard the sound of wheels.

"There," said Richard, feeling the weight of hospitality upon him, "Sophie isn't down.   How like her!"

But at the last moment, to save appearances, Sophie came down the stairs and went into the parlor: indolent, favored Sophie, who always came out right when things looked most against it.

In a little while the empty rooms were peopled. Dress improved the young ladies of the house very much, and the young ladies who came were some of them quite pretty. The gentlemen seemed to me very tiresome and not at all good-looking. Richard was quite a king among them, with his square shoulders, and his tawny moustache, and his blue eyes.

There were not quite gentlemen enough, and Mrs. Hollenbeck fluttered into the library to hunt up Mr. Langenau, and he presently came out with her. He was dressed with more care than usual, and suitably for evening: he had the *vive* attentive manner that is such a contrast to most young men in this country: everybody looked at him and wondered who he was. The music-teacher was playing vigorously, and so, before the German was arranged, several impetuous souls flew away in waltzes up and down the room. The parlor was a very large room. It had originally been two rooms, but had been thrown into one, as some pillars and a slight arch testified. The ceiling was rather low, but the many windows which opened on the piazza, and the unusual size of the room, made it very pretty for a dance. Mary Leighton and the tutor were dancing; somebody was talking to me, but I only saw that.

"How well he dances," I heard some one exclaim.

'I'm afraid it must have been Richard whom I forgot to answer just before: for I saw him twist his yellow moustache into his mouth and bite it; a bad sign with him.

Kilian was to lead with Mary Leighton, and he came up to where we stood, and said to Richard, "I suppose you have Miss Pauline for your partner?"

Now I had been very unhappy for some time, dreading the moment, but there was nothing for it but to tell the truth. So I said, "I hope you are not counting upon me for dancing? You know I cannot dance!"

"Not dance!" cried Kilian, in amazement; "why, I never dreamed of that."

"You don't like it, Pauline?" said Richard, looking at me.

"Like it!" I said, impatiently. "Why, I don't know how; who did I ever have to dance with in Varick-street? Ann Coddle or old Peter? And Uncle Leonard never thought of such a thing as sending me to school."

"Why didn't you tell me before, and we wouldn't have bothered about this stupid dance," said Kilian; but I think he didn't mean it, for he enjoyed dancing very much.

Richard had to go away, for though he hated it, he was needed, as they had not gentlemen enough.

The one or two persons who had been introduced to me, on going to join the dance, also expressed regret. Even Mrs. Hollenbeck came up, and said how sorry she was: she had supposed I danced.

But they all went away, and I was left by one of the furthest windows with a tiresome old man, who didn't dance either, because his legs weren't strong enough, and who talked and talked till I asked him not to; which he didn't seem to like. But to have to talk, with the noise of the music, and the stir of the dancing, and the whirl that is always going on in such a room, is penance. I told him it made my head ache, and besides I couldn't hear, and so at last he went away, and I was left alone.

Sometimes in pauses of the dance Richard came up to me, and sometimes Kilian; but it had the effect of making me more uncomfortable, for it made everybody turn and look at me. Bye and bye I stole away and went on the piazza, and looked in where no one could see me. I could not go away entirely, for I was

5*

fascinated by the dance. I longed so to be dancing, and had such bitter feelings because I never had been taught. After I left the room, I could see Richard was uncomfortable; he looked often at the door, and was not very attentive to his partner. No one else seemed to miss me. Mr. Langenau talked constantly to Miss Lowder, with whom he had been dancing, and never looked once toward where I had been sitting. A long time after, when they had been dancing—hours it seemed to me—Miss Lowder seemed to feel faint or tired, and Mr. Langenau came out with her, and took her up-stairs to the dressing-room.

Ashamed to be seen looking in at the window, I ran into the library and sat down. There was a student's lamp upon the table, but the room had no other light. I sat leaning back in a large chair by the table, with my bouquet in my lap, buttoning and unbuttoning absently my long white gloves. In a moment I heard Mr. Langenau come down-stairs alone: he had left Miss Lowder in the dressing-room to rest there: he came directly toward the library.

He came half-way in the door, then paused. "May I speak to you?" he said slowly, fixing his eyes on mine. "I seem to be the only one who is forbidden, of those who have offended you and of those who have not."

"No one has said what you have," I said very faintly.

In an instant he was standing beside me, with one hand resting on the table.

"Will you listen to me," he said, bending a little toward me and speaking in a quick, low voice, "I did say what you have a right to resent; but I said it in a moment when I was not master of my words. I had just heard something that made me doubt my senses: and my only thought was how to save myself, and not to show how I was staggered by it. I am a proud man, and it is hard to tell you this—but I cannot bear this coldness from you—and *I ask you to forgive me.*"

His eyes, his voice, had all their unconquerable influence upon me. I bent over Richard's poor flowers, and pulled them to pieces while I tried to speak. There was a silence, during which he must have heard the loud beating of my heart, I think: at last he spoke again in a lower voice, "Will you not be kind, and say that we are friends once more?"

I said something that was inaudible to him, and he stooped a little nearer me to catch it. I made a great effort and commanded my voice and said, very low, but with an attempt to speak lightly, "You have not made it any better, but I will forget it."

He caught my hand for one instant, then let it go as suddenly. And neither of us could speak.

There is no position more false and trying than a woman's, when she is told in this way that a man loves her, and yet has not been told it; when she must seem not to see what she would be an idiot not to see; when he can say what he pleases and she must seem to hear only so much. I did no better and no worse than most women of my years would have done. At last the silence (which did not seem a silence to me, it was so full of new and conflicting thoughts,) was broken by the recommencement of the music in the other room. He had taken a book in his hands and was turning over its pages restlessly.

"Why have you not danced?" he said at last, in a voice that still showed agitation.

"I have not danced because I can't, because I never have been taught."

"You? not taught? it seems incredible. But let me teach you. Will you? Teach you! you would dance by intention. And would love it—madly—as I did years ago. Come with me, will you?"

"Oh, no," I said, half frightened, shrinking back, "I am not going to dance—ever."

"Perhaps that is as well," he said in a low tone, meeting my eye for an instant, and telling me by that sudden brilliant gleam from his, that then he would be spared the pain of ever seeing me dancing with another.

" But let me teach you something," he said after a moment. "Let me teach you German—will you ?" He sank down in a chair by the table, and leaning forward, repeated his question eagerly.

" Oh, yes, I should like it so much—if—."

" If—if what ? If it could be arranged without frightening and embarrassing you, you mean ?"

" Yes."

" I wonder if you are not more afraid of being frightened and embarrassed than of any other earthly trial. There are worse things that come to us, Miss d'Estrée. But I will arrange about the German, and you need have no terror. How will I arrange ? No matter—when Mrs. Hollenbeck asks you to join a class in German, you will join it, will you not ?"

" Oh, yes."

" You promise ?"

" Oh, anything."

" Anything ? take care. I may fill up a check for thousands, if you give a blank."

" I didn't give a blank; anything about German's what I meant."

"Ah, that's safer, but not half so generous. And yet you're one who might be generous, I think."

"But tell me about the German class."

"I've nothing to tell you about it," he answered, "only that you've promised to learn."

."But where are we to say our lessons, and what books are we to study?"

"Would you like to say a lesson now and get one step in advance of all the others?"

"O yes! I shall need at least as much grace as that."

"Then say this after me: '*Ich will Alles lernen, was Sie mich lehren.*' Begin. '*Ich will Alles lernen*'—"

"'*Ich will Alles lernen*'—but what does it mean?"

"Oh, that is not important. Learn it first. Can you not trust me? '*Ich will Alles lernen, was Sie mich lehren.*'"

"'*Ich will Alles lernen*'—ah, you look as if my pronunciation were not good."

"I was not thinking of that; you pronounce very well. '*Ich will Alles lernen*—'"

"*Ich will Alles lernen, was Sie mich lehren* :—there *now*, tell me what it means."

"Not until you learn it; *encore une fois.*"

I said it after him again and again, but when I attempted it alone, I made invariably some error.

"Let me write it for you," he said, and pulling a

book from his pocket, tore out a leaf and wrote the sentence on it. "There—keep the paper and study it, and say it to me in the morning."

I have the paper still; long years have passed: it is only a crumpled little yellow fragment; but the world would be poorer and emptier to me if it were destroyed.

I had quite mastered the sentence, saying it after him word for word, and held the slip of paper in my hand, when I heard steps in the hall. I knew Richard's step very well, and gave a little start. Mr. Langenau frowned, and his manner changed, as I half rose from my seat, and as quickly sank back in it again.

"Is it that you lack courage?" he said, looking at me keenly.

"I don't know what I lack," I cried, bending down my head to hide my flushed face; "but I hate to be scolded and have scenes."

"But who has a right to scold you and to make a scene?"

"Nobody: only everybody does it all the same."

"Everybody, I suppose, means Mr. Richard Vandermarck, who is frowning at you this moment from the hall."

"And it means you—who are frowning at me this moment from your seat."

All this time Richard had been standing in the hall; but now he walked slowly away. I felt sure he had given me up. The people began to come out of the parlor, and I felt ready to cry with vexation, when I thought that they would again be talking about me. It was true, I am afraid, that I lacked courage.

"You want me to go away?" he said, fixing his eyes intently on me.

"O yes, if you only would," I said naïvely.

He looked so white and angry when he rose, that I sprang up and put out my hand to stop him, and said hurriedly, "I only meant—that is—I should think you would understand without my telling you. A woman cannot bear to have people talk about her, and know who she likes and who she doesn't. It kills me to have people talk about me. I'm not used to society—I don't know what is right—but I don't think—I am afraid—I ought not to have stayed in here and talked to you away from all the others. It's that that makes me so uncomfortable. That, and Richard too. For I know he doesn't like to have me pleased with any one. Do not go away angry with me. I don't see why you do not understand."

My incoherent little speech had brought him to his senses.

"I am not going away angry," he said in a low voice, "I will promise not to speak to you again to-night. Only remember that I have feelings as well as Mr. Richard Vandermarck."

In a moment more I was alone. Richard did not come near me, nor seem to notice me, as he passed through the hall. Presently Mr. Eugene Whitney came in, and I was very glad to see him.

"Won't you take me to walk on the piazza?" I asked, for everybody else was walking there. He was only too happy; and so the evening ended common-place enough.

CHAPTER X.

She wanted years to understand
The grief that he did feel.

Surrey.

Love is not love
That alters where it alteration finds.

THIS was how the German class was formed.

The next day, as we were leaving the dinner-table, Mr. Langenau paused a few moments by Sophie, in the hall, and talked with her about the boys.

" Charley gets on very well with his German," he observed, "but Benny doesn't make much progress. He is too young to study much, and acquires chiefly by the ear. If you only had a German maid, or if you could speak with him yourself, he would make much better progress."

" Yes, I wish I had more knowledge of the language," she replied; "I read it very easily, but cannot speak with any fluency."

"Why will you never speak it with me ?" he said. "And if you will permit me, I shall be very glad to read with you an hour a day. I have much leisure, and it would be no task to me."

"I should like it very much, and you are very kind. But it is so hard to find an hour unoccupied, particularly with so many people in the house, whom I ought to entertain."

"That is very true, unless you can make it a source of entertainment to them. Miss Benson—is she not a German scholar? She might like to join you."

Then, I think, the clever Sophie's mind was illuminated, and the tutor's little scheme was revealed to her clear eye; she embraced it with effusion. "An admirable idea," she said, "and the others, too, perhaps, would join us if you would not mind. It would be one hour a day at least secure from *ennui:* I shall have great cause to thank you, if we can arrange it. For these girls get so tired of doing nothing; my mind is always on the strain to think of an amusement. Charlotte! Come here, I want to ask you something."

Charlotte Benson came, and with her came Henrietta. I was sitting on the sofa between the parlor-doors, and could not help hearing the whole conversation, as they were standing immediately before me.

"Mr. Langenau proposes to us to read an hour a day with him in German. What do you think about it?"

"Charming," said Charlotte with enthusiasm. "I cannot think of anything that would give me greater pleasure. Henrietta and I have read in German together for two winters, and it will be enchanting to continue it with such a master as Mr. Langenau."

Henrietta murmured her satisfaction, and then Charlotte rushed into plans for the course, leaving me in despair, supposing I' had been forgotten. What place I was to find in such advanced society I could not well imagine.

Mr. Langenau never turned his head in my direction, and talked with Miss Benson with so much earnestness about the books into which they were to plunge, that I could not convince myself that all this was undertaken solely that he might teach me German. In a little while they seemed to have settled it all to their satisfaction, and he had turned to go away. My heart was in my throat. Mrs. Hollenbeck had not forgotten me. She said something low to Mr. Langenau.

"Ah, true!" he said. "But does she know anything of German?" Then turning to me he said, with one of his dazzling sudden glances, "Miss d'Estrée, we are talking of making up a German class; do you understand the language?"

"No," I said, meeting his eye for a moment, "I

have only taken one lesson in my life," and then blushed scarlet at my own audacity.

"Ah," said he, as if quite sorry for the disappointment, "I wish you were advanced enough to join us."

Then Charlotte Benson, quite ignoring the interruption, began to ask him about a book that she wanted very much to find. Mr. Langenau had it in his room—a most happy accident, and there was a great deal said about it. I again was left in doubt of my fate. Again Sophie interposed. "We have forgotten Mary Leighton," she said, gently.

"Does Miss Leighton know anything of German?"

"Not a thing," said Henrietta.

"What does she know anything of, but flirting?" said Charlotte with asperity, glancing out into the grounds where Kilian was murmuring softest folly to her under her pongee parasol.

"Perhaps she'd like to learn," suggested Sophie. "She and Pauline might begin together; that is, if Mr. Langenau would not think it too much trouble to give them an occasional suggestion. And you, Charlotte, I am sure, could help them a great deal."

Charlotte made no disguise of her disinclination to undertake to help them.

Mr. Langenau expressed his willingness so unenthusiastically, that I think Mrs. Hollenbeck was staggered.

I saw her glance anxiously at him, as if to know what really he might mean. She concluded to interpret according to the context, however, and went on.

"But it will be so much better for all to undertake it, if one does. Suppose they try and see how it will work, either before or after our lesson."

"*De tout mon cœur*," said Mr. Langenau, as if, however, his *cœur* had very little interest in the matter.

"Well, about the hour ?" said Charlotte, the woman of business ; "we haven't settled that after all our talking."

There was a great deal more, oh, a great deal more, and then it was settled that five in the afternoon should be considered the German hour—subject to alteration as circumstances should arise.

Mrs. Hollenbeck very discreetly ordered that a beginning should not be made till the next day but one. "The gentlemen will all be here to-morrow, and there may be something else going on." I knew very well she was afraid of Richard, and thought he would not approve her zeal for our improvement.

The first lesson was very dull work for me. It was agreed that Mary Leighton and I should take our lesson after the others, sitting beside them, however, for the benefit of such crumbs of information as might fall to us.

Mr. Langenau took no special notice of me then, and very little that was flattering when Mary Leighton and I began our lesson proper. Mrs. Hollenbeck, Charlotte, and Henrietta took up their books and left, when the infant class was called. I do not think Mr. Langenau took great pains to make the study of the German tongue of interest to Miss Leighton. She was unspeakably bored, and never even learned the alphabet. She was very much unused to mental application, undoubtedly, and was annoyed at appearing dull. There was but one door open to her; to vote German a bore, and give up the class. She made her exit by that door on the occasion of the second lesson, and Mr. Langenau and I were left to pursue our studies undisturbed. The rendezvous was the piazza in fine weather, and the library when it was damp or cloudy. The fidelity with which the senior Germans gathered up their books and left, when their hour was over, was mainly due to the kind thoughtfulness of Mrs. Hollenbeck, who was always prompt, and always found some excuse for carrying away Charlotte and Henrietta with her when she went.

It can be imagined what those hours were to me, those soft, golden afternoons. Sometimes we took our books and went out under the trees to some shaded seats, and sat there till the maid came out to call us in to

tea.   Happy, happy hours in dreamland!   But what
peril to me, and perhaps to him.   It is vain to go
over it all: it is enough that of all the happy days, that
hour from six o'clock till tea-time was the happiest: and
that with strange smoothness, day after day passed on
without bringing interruption to it.   At six the others
went to ride or walk; I was never called, and did not
even wonder at it.

All this time Richard had been going every day to
town and coming back by the evening train.   It was
pretty tiresome work, and he looked rather pale and
worn; but I believe he could not stay away.   I sometimes felt a little sorry when I saw how much he was
out of spirits, but I was in such a happy realm myself,
it did not depress me long: in truth, I forgot it when
he was not actually before me, and sometimes even
then.   "I do not think you are listening to what I
say," he said to me one night as he sat by me in the
parlor.   I blushed desperately, and tried to listen better.   Ah! how often it happened after that.   I blush
again to think how much I pained him, and how silently he bore it all.

The last days of July were very busy ones in the
Wall-street office, and Richard did not give himself
a holiday, till one Saturday, much to be remembered,
the very last day of the month.   I recall with peni-

tence, the impatient feeling that I had when Richard told me he was going to take the day at home. I felt intuitively that it would spoil it all for me. After breakfast, we all played croquet, and then I shut myself into my room with my German books, and selfishly saw no one till dinner. At dinner I was excited and half frightened, as I always was when Mr. Langenau and Richard were both present, and both watching me; it was impossible to please either.

Something was said about the afternoon, and Richard (who all this time knew nothing of the German class) said to me, evidently afraid of some other engagement being entered on, "I hope you will drive with me, Pauline, at five. I ordered the horses when I was down at the stables; I think the afternoon is going to be fine." It was rather a public way of asking one out of so many to go and take a drive; but in truth, Richard was too honest and straightforward to care who knew what he was in pursuit of, and too sore at heart and too indifferent an actor to conceal it if he had desired. But the invitation struck me with such consternation. At five o'clock! The flower and consummation of the day! The hour that I had been looking forward to, since seven the day before. I could not lose it. I would not go to drive. I hated Richard. I hated going to drive. I grew very brave, and was on the point of saying that I could not go, when I caught Sophie's eye. She made me a quick sign, which I dared not disobey. I blushed crimson, and did not lift my eyes again, but said in a low voice that I would go. Then my heart seemed to turn to lead, and all the glory and pleasure of the day was gone. It seemed to me of such vast importance, of such endless duration, this penance that I was to undergo. O lovers! Foolish, foolish men and women! I was like a child balked of its holiday; I wanted to cry—I longed to get away by myself. I did not dare to look at any one.

Mr. Langenau excused himself, and left the table before the others went away. As we were leaving the table, Sophie, passing close by me, said quite low, "I would not say anything about the German class, Pauline. And it was a great deal better that you should go; you know Richard has not many holidays."

"Yes, but you don't give up all your pleasures for him," I thought, but did not say.

I went quickly to my room, and saw no one till I came down-stairs at five o'clock. I had on a veil, for my face was rather flushed, and my eyes somewhat the worse for crying. Richard was waiting for me at the foot of the stairs, and accompanied me silently to

the wagon, which stood at the door. As we passed
the parlor I could see, on the east piazza, Mr. Langenau
and Charlotte already at their books. Both were so
engrossed that they did not look up as we went
through the hall. For that, Richard, poor fellow! had
to suffer. I was too unreasonable to comprehend that
Mr. Langenau's absorbed manner was a covering for
his pique. It was enough torture to have to lose my
lesson, without seeing him engrossed with some one
else, whose fate was happier than mine. Perhaps,
after all, he was fascinated by Charlotte Benson. She
was bright, clever, and understood him so well. She
admired him so much. She was, I was sure, half in
love with him. (The day before I had concluded she
liked Richard very much.) That was a very disagreeable drive. I complained of the heat. The sun hurt
my eyes.

"We can go back, if you desire it," said Richard,
with a shade of sternness in his voice, stopping the
horses suddenly, after two miles of what would have
been ill-temper if we had been married, but was now
perhaps only petulance.

"I don't desire it," I said, quite frightened, "but I
do wish we could go a little faster till we get into the
shade."

After that, there was naturally very little pleasure

in conversation. I felt angry with Richard and ashamed of myself. For him, I am afraid his feelings were very bitter, and his silence the cover of a sore heart. We had started to take a certain drive; we both wished it over, I suppose, but both lacked courage to shorten it, or go home before we were expected. There was a brilliant sunset, but I am sure we did not see it: then the clouds gathered and the twilight came on, and we were nearly home.

"Pauline," said Richard, hoarsely, not looking at me, and insensibly slackening the hold he had upon the reins; "will you let me say something to you? I want to give you some advice, if you will listen to me."

"I don't want anybody to advise me," I said in alarm, " and I don't know what right you have to expect me to listen to you, Richard, unless it is that I am your guest; and I shouldn't think that was any reason why I should be made to listen to what isn't pleasant to me."

The horses started forward, from the sudden emphasis of Richard's pull upon the reins; and that was all the answer that I had to my most unjustifiable words. Not a syllable was spoken after that; and in a few moments we were at the house. Richard silently handed me out; if I had been thinking about him I should have been frightened at the expression of his face, but I was not: I was only thinking—that we were at home, and that I was going to have the happiness of meeting Mr. Langenau.

CHAPTER XI.

SOPHIE'S WORK.

A nature half transformed, with qualities
That oft betrayed each other, elements
Not blent, but struggling, breeding strange effects
Passing the reckoning of his friends or foes.

George Eliot.

High minds of native pride and force
Most deeply feel thy pangs, remorse!
Fear for their scourge, mean villains have,
Thou art the torturer of the brave.

Scott.

THIS was what Sophie had done: she had invoked forces that she could not control, and she felt, as people are apt to feel when they watch their monster growing into strength, a little frightened and a little sorry. No doubt it had seemed to her a very small thing, to favor the folly of a girl of seventeen, fascinated by the voice and manner of a nameless stranger; it was a folly most manifest, but she had nothing to do with it, and was not responsible; a very small thing to allow, and to encourage what, doubtless, she flattered herself, her discouragement could not have subdued.

It was very natural that she should not wish Richard to marry any one; she was not more selfish than most sisters are. Most sisters do not like to give their brothers up. She would have to give up her home (one of her homes, that is,) as well. She did not think Richard's choice a wise one: she was not subject to the fascination of outline and coloring that had subjugated him, and she felt sincerely that she was the best judge. If Richard must marry (though in thinking of her own married life, she could not help wondering why he must), let him marry a woman who had fortune, or position, or talent. Of course there was a chance that this one might have money, but that would be according to the caprice of a selfish old man, who had never been known to show any affection for her.

But money was not what Richard wanted: his sister knew much better what Richard wanted, than he knew himself. He wanted a clever woman, a woman who would keep him before the world and rouse him into a little ambition about what people thought of him. Sophie was disappointed and a little frightened when she found that Richard did not give up the outline and coloring pleasantly. She had thought he would be disillusionized, when he found he was thrown over for a German tutor, who could sing.

She had not counted upon seeing him look ill and worn, and finding him stern and silent to her; to her, of whom he had always been so fond. She found he was taking the ‑matter very seriously, and she almost wished that she had not meddled with the matter.

And this German tutor—who could sing—well, it was strange, but he was the worst feature of her Frankenstein, and the one at which she felt most sorry and most frightened. Richard was very bad, to be sure, but he would no doubt get over it: and if it all came out well, she would be the gainer. As to "this girl for whom his heart was sick," she had no manner of patience with her or pity for her.

"She must suffer: so do all;" she would undoubtedly have a hard future, no matter to which of these men who were so absurd about her, Fate finally accorded her: hard, if she married Richard without loving him (nobody knew better than Sophie how hard that sort of marriage was); hard, if she married the German, to suffer a lifetime of poverty and ill-temper and jealous fury. But about all that, Sophie did not care a straw. She knew how much women could live through, and it seemed to be their business to be wretched.

But this man! And she could not gain anything by what he suffered, with his dangerous nature, his

ungovernable jealousy, his possibly involved and unknown antecedents; what was to become of him, in
case he could not have this girl of whom six weeks
ago he had not heard? A pretty candidate to present
to "mon oncle" of the Wall-street office, for the hand
of the young lady trusted to their hospitality—a very
pretty candidate—a German tutor—who could sing.
If he took her, it was to be feared he would have to
take her without more dowry than some very heavy
imprecations. But could he take her, even thus?
Sophie had some very strange misgivings. This man
was desperately unhappy: was suffering frightfully:
it made her heart ache to see the haggard lines deep-
ening on his face, to see his colorless lips and restless
eyes. She was sorry for him, as a woman is apt to be
sorry for a fascinating man. And then she was
frightened, for he was "no carpet knight so trim," to
whom cognac, and cigars, and time would be a balm:
this man was essentially dramatic, a dangerous character, an article with which she was unfamiliar. He
was frantic about this silly girl: that was plain to see.
Why then was he so wretched, seeing she was as irra-
tionally in love with him?

"If it only comes out right," she sighed distrustfully
many times a day. She resolved never to interfere
with anything again, but it came rather late, seeing

6*

she probably had done the greatest mischief that she
ever would be permitted to have a hand in while she
lived.   She made up her mind not to think anything
about it, but, unfortunately for that plan, she could
not get out of sight of her work. If she had been a
man, she would probably have gone to the Adiron-
dacks.   But being a woman she had to stay at home,
and sit down among the tangled skeins which she had
not skill to straighten.

"If it only comes out right," she sighed again,
the evening of that most uncomfortable drive, "If it
only comes out right."   But it did not look much
like it.

I had gone directly in to tea, and so had Richard.
Richard's face silenced and depressed everybody at the
table; and Mr. Langenau did not come.

"There is going to be a terrible shower," said some
one, and before the sentence was ended, there was a
vivid flash of lightning that made the candles
pale.

"How rapidly it has come up," said Sophie. "Was
the sky black when you came in, Richard?"

"I do not know," said Richard, and nobody doubted
that he told the truth.

"It had begun to darken before we came up from
the river," said Charlotte Benson.   "The clouds were

rising rapidly as we came in. It will be a fearful tempest."

" Are the windows all shut?" said Sophie to the servant.

" I should think so," exclaimed Kilian. " The heat is horrid."

" Yes, it is suffocating," said Richard, getting up.

As he went out of the dining-room, some one, I think Henrietta, said, " Well, I hope Mr. Langenau will get in safely; he was out on the river when we were on the hill."

The storm was so sudden and so furious that everybody was concerned at hearing this; even Kilian made some exclamation of alarm.

" Does he know anything about a boat?" he asked of Richard, who had paused in the doorway, hearing what was said.

" I have no idea," said Richard, shortly, but he did not go away.

" It isn't the sail-boat that he has, of course," said Kilian, thoughtfully. " He always goes out to row, I believe."

" Why, no," said Charlotte Benson, "he's in the sail-boat; don't you remember saying, Henrietta, how bright the gleam of the sunset was on the sail, and all the water was so dark?"

Kilian came to his feet very suddenly at these words.

"That's a bad business," he said quickly to his brother. "I've no idea he can manage her in such a squall."

Sophie gave a little scream, and Charlotte and Henrietta both grew very pale, as a frightful shock of thunder followed. The wind was furious, and the unfastened shutters in various parts of the house sounded like so many reports of pistols, and in an instant the whole force of the rain fell suddenly and at once upon the windows. Somewhere some glass was shattered, and all these sounds added to the sense of danger, and the darkness was so great and so sudden, that it was difficult to realize that half an hour before, the sunset could have whitened the sails of a boat upon the river.

"I'm afraid it's too late to do much now," said Kilian, stopping in front of his brother in the doorway.

"What's the use of talking in that way," returned Richard in a hoarse, low voice. "If you hav'nt more sense than to talk so before women, you can stay at home with them," he continued, striding across the hall, and picking up a lantern that stood in a corner near the door. Charlotte Benson caught up one of the candles from the table, and ran to him and lit the lamp within the lantern. Sophie threw a cloak over Kilian's shoulders, and Henrietta flew to carry a message to the kitchen. Richard pulled a bell that was a signal to the stable (the stable was very near the house), and in almost a moment's time two men, beside Kilian, were following him out into the tempest. We saw their lanterns flicker for an instant, and then they were swallowed up in the darkness. The fury of the storm increased every moment. The flashes of lightning were but a few seconds apart, and the roll of thunder was incessant. Every few moments, above this continued roar, would come an appalling crash which sounded just above our heads. The children were screaming with fear, the servants had come into the hall and seemed in a helpless sort of panic. Sophie was very pale and Mary Leighton clung hysterically to her. Charlotte Benson was the only one who seemed to be self-possessed enough to have done anything, if there had been anything to do. But there was not. All we could do was to try to behave ourselves with fortitude in view of the personal danger, and with composure in view of that of others. Presently there came a lull in the tempest, and we began to breathe freer; some one went to the door and opened it. A gust of cold wind swept through the hall and put out the lamp, at which the chil-

dren and Mary Leighton renewed their cries of
fright.

The respite in the tempest was but temporary; before the lamp was relit and order restored, the storm
had burst again upon us. This was, if anything, fiercer,
but shorter lived. After fifteen or twenty minutes'
rage, it subsided almost utterly, and we could hear it
taking itself off across the heavens. I suppose the
whole storm, from its beginning to its end, had not
occupied more than three quarters of an hour, but it
had seemed much longer.

We were very glad to open the door and let the
cool, damp air into the hall. The children were taken
up-stairs, consoled with the promise that word should
be sent to them when their uncles should return.
The servants went feebly off to their domain; one
was sent to sweep the piazza, for the rain had beaten
in such torrents upon it that it was impossible to walk
there, till it should be brushed away. Wrapped in
their shawls, Henrietta and Charlotte Benson walked
up and down the space that the servant swept, and
watched and listened for a long half-hour. I took a
cloak from the rack and, leaning against the door-post,
stood and listened silently.

From the direction of the river there was nothing
to be heard. There was still distant thunder, but

that was the only sound, that and the dripping of the
rain off the leaves of the drenched trees. The wind
was almost silent, and in the spaces of the broken
clouds there were occasional faint stars. A fine,
young tree, uprooted by the tempest, lay across the
carriage-way before the house, its topmost branches
resting on the steps of the piazza: the grass was
strewed with leaves like autumn, and the paths were
simply pools of water. Sophie, more than once, came
to the door, and begged us to come in, for fear of the
dampness and the cold, but no one heeded her suggestion. Even she herself came out very often, and
looked and listened anxiously. Finally my ear caught
a sound: I ran down the steps, and bent forward
eagerly. There was some one coming along the
garden-path that led up from the river. I could hear
the water plashing as he walked, and he was coming
rapidly. In a moment the others heard it too, and
starting to the steps, stood still, and waited breathlessly. He had no lantern, for we could have seen
that; he was almost at the steps before I could re-
cognize him. It was Richard. I gave a smothered
cry, and springing forward, held out my hands to
stop him.

"Tell me what has happened." He put aside my
hands, and went past me without a second look.

" There has nothing happened, but what he can tell you when he comes," he said, as he strode past me up the steps, and on into the house.   Then he was alive to tell me: the reaction was a little too strong for me, and I sat down on the steps to try and recover myself, for I was ill and giddy.

In a few moments more, more steps sounded in the distance, this time slowly, several persons coming together.   I started and ran up the steps, I don't exactly know why, and stood behind the others, who were crowding down, servants and all, to hear what was the news.   Kilian came first, very drenched, and spattered, and subdued looking, then Mr. Langenau, leaning upon one of the men, very pale, but making an attempt to smile and speak reassuringly to Sophie, who met him with looks of great alarm.   It evidently gave him dreadful pain to move, and when he reached the house he was quite faint.   Charlotte Benson placed a chair, into which they supported him.

" Run, Pauline, and get some brandy," said Sophie, putting a bunch of keys into my hand without looking at me.

When I came back with the glass of brandy, he was conscious again, and looked at me and took the glass from my hand.   The other man had been sent for the doctor from the village, who was expected

every moment, and Mr. Langenau, who was now revived by stimulants, was quite reassuring, and attempted to laugh at us for being so much frightened.
Then the young ladies' curiosity got the better of
their terror, and they clamored for the history of the
past two hours. . This history was given them prin-
cipally by Kilian. I cannot repeat it satisfactorily, for
the reason that I don't know anything about jibs, and
bowsprits, and masts, and centre-boards, and I did not
understand it at the time; but I received enough out
of the mass of evidence presented in that language,
to be sure that there had been considerable danger,
and that everybody had behaved well. In fact,
Kilian's changed manner toward the tutor of itself
was quite enough to show that he had behaved unexpectedly well.

The unvarnished and unbowspritted and unjib-
boomed tale was pretty much as follows : Mr. Langenau
had found himself in the middle of the river, when the
storm came on. I am afraid he could not have been
thinking very much about the clouds, not to have noticed that a storm was rising ; though every one agreed
that they had never known anything like the rapidity
of its coming up. Before he knew what he was about,
a squall struck him, and he had great difficulty to
right the boat. (Then followed a good deal about

luffing and tacking and keeping her taut to wind-
ward; that is, I think that was where he wanted to
keep her.) But whatever it was, he didn't succeed in
doing it, and Kilian vouchsafed to say nobody could
have done it. Then something split: I really cannot
say whether it was the mast, or the bowsprit, or the
centre-board, but whatever it was, it hurt Mr. Langenau so much that for a moment he was stunned. And
then Kilian cannot see why he wasn't drowned.
When he came to himself he was still holding the rudder in his hand.

The other arm was useless from the falling of—this
thing that split—upon it. And so the boat was
floundering about in the gale till it got righted, and
it was Mr. Langenau's presence of mind that saved
him and the boat, for he never let go the rudder, and
controlled her as far as he could, though he did not
know where he was going, the blackness was so great,
and the flashes did not show him the shore; and he
was like one placed in the midst of a frightful sea
wakened out of a dream, owing to the blow and the
unconsciousness which followed.

Then Richard came upon the stage as hero; he and
one of the men had gone out in the only boat at hand,
a very small one, toward the speck, which, by the
flashes of lightning, he saw out upon the river. It was

almost impossible to overhaul her, and it could not have been done at the rate she was going, of course; but then occurred that accident which rendered Mr. Langenau unconscious, and which brought things to a standstill for a moment. Kilian said we did not know anything about the storm up here at the house; that more than one tree had been struck within a few feet of him on the shore. The river was surging; the wind was furious; no one could imagine what it was who had not witnessed it, and he, for his part, never expected to see Richard come back to land. But Richard did come back, and brought back the disabled sail-boat and the injured man. That was the end of the story; which thrilled us all very much, as we knew the heroes, and had one of them before us, ghastly pale but uncomplaining.

It seemed as if the doctor never would come! We were women, and we naturally looked to the coming of the doctor as the end of all the trouble. It was impossible to make the poor fellow comfortable. He could not lie down, he could not move without excruciating pain, and very frequently he grew quite faint. Charlotte Benson and Sophie administered stimulants; endeavored to ease his position with pillows and footstools; and did all the nameless soothing acts that efficient and good nurses alone understand; while I, paralyzed and mute, stood aside, scarcely able to bear the sight of his sufferings. I am sorry to say, I don't think he cared at all to have me by him. He was in such pain that he cared only for the attendance of those who could alleviate it in a measure; and the strong firm hand and the skilled touch were more to him than the presence of one who had nothing but excited and unavailing sympathy to offer. It was rather a stern fact walking into my dreamland, this.

By and bye Kilian went away to take off his wet clothes, and he did not come back again, but sent down a message to his sister that he was very tired and should go to bed, but if he were wanted for anything he could be called. This was not heroic of Kilian, but, after the manner of men, he was apt to keep away from the sight of disagreeable things.

After all, he could not do much good, but it was something to feel there was a man to call upon, besides Patrick, who was stupid; and I saw Charlotte Benson's lip curl when Kilian's message was brought down.

Richard was in his room: we all thought he had done enough for one night, and had a right to rest.

At last, after the most weary waiting, wheels were heard, and the doctor drove up to the door. The servants had begun to look very sleepy. Mary Leighton had slipped away to her room, and Sophie had told Henrietta and me to go, for we were really of no earthly use. We did not take her advice as a compliment, and did not go. Henrietta opened the door for the doctor, which was doing something though not much, as two of the maids stood prepared to do it if she did not.

The doctor was a reassuring, quiet man, and became a pillar of strength at once. After talking a few moments with Mr. Langenau, and pulling and twisting him rather ruthlessly, he walked a little away with Sophie, and told her he wanted him got at once to his room, and he should need the assistance of one of the gentlemen. Would not Patrick do? Besides Patrick. Mr. Langenau's shoulder was dislocated, badly, and it must be set at once. It was a painful operation and he needed help. I was within hearing of this, and I was in great alarm. Sophie looked so too, and I don't think she liked disagreeable things any better than her brother, but she was a woman, and could not shirk them as he could.

"Pauline," she said, finding me at her side as she turned, "run up and tell Richard that he must come down, quick. Tell him how it is, and that he must make haste."

I ran up the stairs breathlessly, but feeling all the

time that it was rather hard that I must be sent to
Richard with this message. Sophie did not want to
ask him to come down herself, and she thought me
the most likely ambassador to bring him, but it was
not a congenial embassy. Perhaps, however, she
only asked me because I happened to be nearest
her, and she was rather upset by what the doctor
said.

I knocked at Richard's door.

" Well ?"

" Oh, they want you to come down-stairs a minute.
There's something to be done," panting and rather
incoherent.

" What is to be done ?"

" The Doctor's here, and he says he must have
help."

" Where's Kilian ?"

" Gone to bed."

Some suppressed ejaculation, and he pushed back
his chair, and rose, and came across the room : at
least it sounded so, and I ran down the stairs again.
He followed me in a moment. The Doctor came forward and talked to him a little while, and then
Richard called Patrick, and told Sophie to see that
Mr. Langenau's room was ready.

" How can he get up two pairs of stairs," said

Charlotte Benson, " when he cannot move an inch without such suffering ?"

" That's very true," the Doctor said. " I doubt if he could bear it. You have no room below ?"

" Put a bed in the library," said Charlotte Benson, and in ten minutes it was done; the servants no longer sleepy when they had any definite order to fulfill.

" In the meantime," said Richard to his sister, " send those two to bed," pointing out Henrietta and me.

" I've told them to go, but they won't," said Sophie, somewhat sharply.

Henrietta walked off, rather injured, but I would not go.

Mr. Langenau had another faint attack, and I was quite certain he would die. Charlotte was making him breathe *sal volatile* and Sophie ran to rub his hands. The Doctor was busy at the light about something.

" The room is all ready," said the servant.

" Very well; now Mr. Richard, if you please," the Doctor said.

" Pauline," said Richard, coming to me as I stood at the foot of the balusters, " You can't do any good. You'd better go up-stairs."

"Oh, Richard," I cried, "I think you're very cruel; I think you might let me stay."

I suppose my wretchedness, and youthfulness, and folly softened him again, and he said, very gently, "I don't mean to be unkind, but it is best for you to go. You need not be so frightened: there isn't any danger."

I moved slowly to obey him, but turned back and caught his hand and whispered, "You won't let them hurt him, Richard?" and then ran up the stairs. No doubt Richard thought I went to my own room; but I spent the next hour on the landing-place, looking down into the hall.

It was rather a serious matter, getting Mr. Langenau even into the library, and it was well they had not attempted his own room. Patrick was called, and with his assistance and Richard's, he began to move across the hall. But half-way to the library-door, he fainted dead away, and Richard carried him and laid him on the bed, Patrick being worse than useless, having lost his head, and the Doctor being a small man, and only strong in science.

Pretty soon the library-door closed, and Sophie and Charlotte were excluded. They walked about the hall, talking in low tones, and looking anxious. Later, there came groaning from within the closed door, and Charlotte Benson wrung her hands and listened. The groans continued for a long while: the misery of hearing them! After a while they ceased: then Richard opened the door, hastily, it seemed, and called "Sophie."

Sophie ran forward, and the door closed again. There was a long silence, time enough for those who were outside to imagine all manner of horrid possibilities. Then the Doctor and Richard came out.

"How is he, Doctor?" said Charlotte Benson, bravely, going to meet them, while I hung trembling over the landing-place.

"Oh better, better, very comfortable," said the Doctor, in his calm professional tone.

I could not help thinking those groans had not denoted a very high state of comfort; but maybe the Doctor knew best how people with dislocated shoulders and broken ribs are apt to express their sentiments of satisfaction.

I listened with more than interest to their plans for the night: the Doctor was going away at once; two of the servants and Patrick were to relieve each other in sitting by him, while Richard was to throw himself on the sofa in the hall, to be at hand if anything were needed.

"Which means, that you are to be awake all night,"

7

said Charlotte Benson. "You have more need of rest than we. Let Sophie and me take your place."

Richard looked gratefully and kindly at her, but refused. The Doctor assured them again that there was no reason for anxiety; that Richard would probably be undisturbed all night; that he himself would come early in the morning. Then Richard came toward the stairs, and I escaped to my own room.

CHAPTER XII.

PRÆMONITUS, PRÆMUNITUS.

The fiend whose lantern lights the mead,
Were better mate than I !
Scott.

Fools, when they cannot see their way,
At once grow desperate,
Have no resource—have nothing to propose—
But fix a dull eye of dismay
Upon the final close.
Success to the stout heart, say I,
That sees its fate, and can defy !
Faust.

Two weeks later, and things had not stood still;
they rarely do, when there is so much at hand, and
ripe for mischief; seventeen does not take up the
practice of wisdom voluntarily. I do not think I was
very different from other girls of seventeen, and I
cannot blame myself very much that I spent all these
days in a dream of bliss and folly; how could it have
been otherwise, situated exactly as we were ? This is
the way our days were passed. Mr. Langenau was
better, but still not able to leave his room. He was

the hero, as a matter of course, and little besides his sufferings, his condition, and his prospects, was talked of at the table; which had the effect of making Kilian stay away two nights out of three, and of alienating Richard altogether. Richard went to town on Monday morning after the accident occurred, and it was now Friday of the following week, and he had not come back.

It was a little dull for Mary Leighton and for Henrietta, perhaps; possibly for Charlotte Benson, but she did not seem to mind it much; and I had never found R—— so enchanting as that fortnight. Charlotte Benson liked to be Florence Nightingale in little, it was very plain; and naturally nothing made me so happy as to be permitted to minister to the wants of the (it must be confessed) frequently unreasonable sufferer. For the first few days, while he was confined to his bed, of course Charlotte and I were obliged to content ourselves with the sending of messages, the arranging of bouquets, the concocting of soups and jellies, and all the other coddling processes at our command. But when Mr. Langenau was able to sit up, Sophie (at the instance of Charlotte Benson, for she seemed to have renounced diplomacy herself,) arranged that the bed should be taken away during the daytime, and brought back again at night, and that Mr. Langenau should lie on the sofa through the day. This made it possible for us to be in the room, even without Sophie, though we began to think her presence necessary. That scruple was soon done away with, for it laid too great a tax on her, and restricted our attentions very much. The result was, we passed nearly the whole day beside him; Mary Leighton and Henrietta very often of the party, and Sophie occasionally looking in upon us. Sometimes when Charlotte Benson, as ranking officer, decreed that the patient needed rest, we took our books and work and went to the piazza, outside the window of his room.

He would have been very tired of us, if he had not been very much in love with one of us. As it was, it must have been a kind of fool's paradise in which he lived, five pretty women fluttering about him, offering the prettiest homage, and one of them the woman for whom, wisely or foolishly, rightly or wrongly, he had conceived so violent a passion.

As soon as he was out of pain and began to recover the tone of his nerves at all, I saw that he wanted me beside him more than ever, and that Charlotte Benson, with all her skill and cleverness, was as nothing to him in comparison. No doubt he dissembled this with care; and was very graceful and very grateful and infinitely interesting. His moods were very varying, however; sometimes he seemed struggling with the most unconquerable depression, then we were all so sorry for him; sometimes he was excited and brilliant; then we were all thrilled with admiration. And not unfrequently he was irritable and quite morose and sullen. And then we pitied, and admired, and feared him *à la fois.* I am sure no man more fitted to command the love and admiration of women ever lived.

Charlotte Benson with great self-devotion had insisted upon teaching the children for two hours every day, so that Mr. Langenau might not be annoyed at the thought that they were losing time, and that Sophie might not be inconvenienced. It was the least that she could do, she reasoned, after the many lessons that Mr. Langenau had given us, with so much kindness, and without accepting a return. Henrietta volunteered for the service, also, and from eleven to one every day the boys were caught and caged, and made to drink at the fountain of learning ; or rather to approach that fountain, of which forty Charlottes and Henriettas could not have made them drink.

At that time Charlotte always decreed that Mr. Langenau should lie on the sofa and go to sleep. The windows were darkened, and the room was cleared of visitors. On this Friday morning, nearly two weeks after the accident, as I was following Sophie from the room (Charlotte having gone with Henrietta to capture the children), Mr. Langenau called after me rather imperiously, "Miss d'Estrée—Miss Pauline—"

It had béen a stormy session, and I turned back with misgivings. Sophie shrugged her shoulders and went away toward the dining-room.

"What are you going away for, may I ask ?" he said, as I appeared before him humbly.

"Why, you know you ought to lie down and to rest," I tried to say with discretion, but it was all one what I said : it would have irritated him just the same.

"I am rather tired of this surveillance," he exclaimed. "It is almost time I should be permitted to express a wish about the disposition of myself. As I do not happen to want to go to sleep, I beg I may be allowed the pleasure of your society for a little while."

"I don't think it would give you much pleasure, and you know you don't feel as well to-day."

"Again, may I be permitted to judge how I feel myself ?"

"Oh, yes, of course, but—"

"But what, Miss d'Estrée ?—No doubt you want to go yourself—I am sorry I thought of detaining you (with a gesture of dismissal). I beg you to excuse me. A sick man is apt to be unreasonable."

"Oh, as to that, you know entirely well I do not want to go. You are unreasonable, indeed, when you talk as you do now. I only went away for your benefit."

"*Qui s'excuse, s'accuse.*"

"But I am not excusing myself; and if you put it so I will go away at once."

"*Si vous voulez—*"

"But I don't '*voulez*'—Oh, how disagreeable you can be."

"You will stay ?"

"Pauline !" called Sophie from across the hall.

"There !" I exclaimed, interpreting it as the voice of conscience. I left my work-basket and book upon the table, and went out of the room.

"You called me ?" I said, following her into the parlor, where, shutting the door, she motioned me to a seat beside her. She had a slip of paper and an envelope in her hand, and seemed a little ill at ease.

"I've just had a telegram from Richard," she said. "He's coming home to-night by the eleven o'clock train. It's so odd altogether. I don't know why he's coming. But you may as well read his message yourself," she said with a forced manner, handing me the paper. It was as follows :

"Send carriage for me to eleven-thirty train to-night. Remember my injunctions, our last conversation, and your promises."

" Well ?" I said, looking up, bewildered and not violently interested, for I was secretly listening to the quick shutting of the library-door.

" Why, you see," she returned, with a forced air of confidence that made me involuntarily shrink from her ; I think she even laid her hand upon my sleeve, or made some gesture of familiarity which was unusual—

" You see, that last conversation was—about you. Richard is annoyed at—at your intimacy with Mr. Langenau. You know just as well as I do how he feels, for no doubt he's spoken to you himself."

" He never has," I said, quite shortly.

" No ?" and she looked rather chagrined. " Well— but at all events you know how he feels. Girls ar'nt slow generally to find out about those things. And he is really very unhappy about it, very. I wish, Pauline, you'd give it up, child. It's gone quite far enough ; now don't you think so yourself? Mr. Langenau isn't the sort of man to be serious about, you know. It's all very well, just for a summer's amusement. But, you know, you mustn't go too far. I'm sure, dear, you're not angry with me : now you understand just what I mean, don't you ?"

7*

No: not angry, certainly not angry. She went on, still with the impertinent touch upon my arm: " Richard made me promise that I would look after you, and not permit things to go too far. And you see—well—I'll tell you in confidence what I think his coming to-night means, and his message and all. I think—that is, I am afraid—he's found out something against Mr. Langenau - since he's been away. I know he never has felt confidence in him. But I've always thought, perhaps that was because he was—well—a little jealous and suspicious. You know men are so apt to be suspicious; and I was sure, when he went away that last Monday morning, that he would not leave a stone unturned in finding out everything . about him. It is that that's kept him, I am sure. Don't let that make you feel hardly toward Richard," she went on, noticing perhaps my look; " you know it's only natural, and besides, it's right. How would he answer to your uncle ?"

" It is I who should answer to my uncle," I re-turned, under my breath.

" Yes, but you are in our house, in our care. You know, my dear child, you are very young and very inexperienced; you don't know how very careful people have to be."

" Why don't you talk that way to Charlotte and

Henrietta and Mary Leighton? Have I done anything so very different from them?" I answered, with
a blaze of spirit.

"No, dear," she said, with a little laugh, "only
there are one or two men very much in love with
you, and that makes everything so different."

I blushed scarlet, and was silenced instantly, as she
intended.

"Now, maybe I am mistaken about his having
discovered something," she went on, "but I can't
make anything else out of Richard's message. He is
not one to send off such a despatch without a reason.
Evidently he is very uneasy; and I thought it was
best to be perfectly frank with you, dear, and I know
you'll do me the justice to say I have been, if Richard
ever says anything to you about it. You mustn't
blame me, you know, for the way he feels. I wish
the whole thing was at an end," she said, with the
first touch of sincerity. "And now promise me one
thing," with another caressing movement of the hand,
"Promise me, you won't go into the library again till
Richard comes, and we hear what he has to say.
Just for my sake, you know, my dear, for you see he
would blame me if I did not keep a strict surveillance. You won't mind doing that, I'm sure, for
me?"

"I shall not promise anything," I returned, getting up, "but I am not likely to go near the library after what you've said."

"That's a good child," she said, evidently much relieved, and thinking that the affair was very near its end. I opened the door, and she added: "Now go up-stairs, and rest yourself, for you look as if you had a headache, and don't think of anything that's disagreeable." That was a good prescription, but I did not take it.

Of course, I did not go near the library; that was understood. After dinner, the servant brought in Mr. Langenau's tray untouched, and Charlotte Benson started up, and ran in to see what was the matter. Sophie went too, looking a little troubled. I think they were both snubbed: for ten minutes after, when I met Charlotte in the hall, she had an unusual flush upon her cheek, and Sophie I found standing at one of the parlor-windows, biting her lip, and tapping impatiently upon the carpet. Evidently the affair was not as near its placid end as she had hoped. She started a little when she saw me, and tried to look unruffled.

"How sultry it is this afternoon!" she said. "Are you going up to your room to take a rest? stop in my room on your way, I want to show you those embroideries that I was telling Charlotte Benson of last night."

"I did not hear you, and I do not know anything about them," I said, feeling not at all affectionate.

"No? Oh, I forgot: it was while you and Henrietta were sitting in the library, and Charlotte and I were walking up and down the piazza while it rained. Why, they are some heavenly sets that I got this spring from Paris—Marshall picked them up one day at the *Bon Marché*—and verily they are *bon marché*. I never saw anything so cheap, and I was telling Charlotte that some of you might just as well have part of them, for I never could use the half. Come up and look them over."

Now I loved "heavenly sets" as well as most women, but dress was not the bait for me at that moment. So I said my head ached and I could not look at them then, if she'd excuse me; and I went silently away to my room, not caring at all if she were pleased or not. I disliked and distrusted her more and more every moment, and she seemed to me so mean: for I knew all her worry came from the apprehension of what she might have to fear from Richard, not the thought of the suffering that he or that any one else endured.

It was a long afternoon, but it reached its end,

after the manner of all afternoons on record, even those of Marianna. When I came down-stairs they were all at tea and Kilian had arrived. A more enlivening atmosphere prevailed, and the invalid was not discussed. A drive was being canvassed. There was an early moon, and Kilian proposed driving Tom and Jerry before the open wagon, which would carry four, through the valley-road, to be back by half-past nine or ten o'clock.

" But what am I to do," cried Kilian, " when there are five angels, and I have only room for three ?"

" Why, two will have to stay at home, according to my arithmetic," said Charlotte, good-naturedly, " and I've no doubt I shall be remainder."

" If you stay, I shall stay with you," said Henrietta, dropping the metaphor, for metaphors, even the mildest, were beyond her reach of mind.

Everybody wanted to stay, and everybody tried to be quite firm ; but as no one's firmness but mine was based on inclination, the result was that Sophie and I were " remainder," and Mary Leighton, Charlotte, and Henrietta drove away with Kilian quite jauntily, at half-past seven o'clock. But before she went, Charlotte, who was really good-natured with all her sharpness and self-will, went into the library to speak to Mr. Langenau, and to show she did not resent the noonday slight, whatever that had been. But presently she came back looking rather anxious, and said to Sophie, ignoring me (whom she always did ignore if possible),

" Do go and see what you can do for Mr. Langenau. He is really very far from well. His tea stands there, . and he hasn't taken anything to eat. He looks feverish and excited, and I truly think he ought to see the Doctor. You know he promised the Doctor to stay in his room, and keep still all the rest of the week. But I am sure he means to come out to-morrow, and he even talks of going down to town. It will kill him if he does; I'm sure he's doing badly, and I wish you'd go and see to him."

" Does he know Richard is coming up to-night?" asked Sophie, *sotto voce*, but with affected carelessness.

" I do not know; oh yes, he does, I mentioned it to him at dinner-time, I remember now."

" Well, I'll see if I can do anything for him; now go, they're waiting for you. Have a pleasant time."

After they were gone, Sophie went into the library, but she did not stay very long. She came and sat beside me on the river-balcony, and talked a little, desultorily and absent-mindedly.

Presently there was a call for " mamma," a hubbub and a hurry—soon explained. Charley, who had been

running wild for the last two weeks, without tutor or
uncle to control him, had just fallen from the mow,
and hurt himself somewhat, and frightened himself
much more. The whole house was in a ferment. He
was taken to mamma's room, for he was a great baby
when anything was the matter with him, and would
not let mamma move an inch away from him. After
assisting to the best of my ability in making him
comfortable, and seeing myself only in the way, I
went down-stairs again, and took my seat upon the
balcony that overlooked the river.

The young moon was shining faintly, and the air
was soft and balmy. The house was very still; the
servants, I think, were all in a distant part of the house,
or out enjoying the moonlight and the idleness of
evening. Sophie was nailed to Charley's bed up-
stairs, trying to soothe him; Benny was sinking to
sleep in his little crib. It seemed like an enchanted
palace, and when I heard a step crossing the parlor, it
made me start with a vague feeling of alarm. The
parlor-window by me, which opened to the floor, was
not closed, and in another moment some one came
out and stood beside me. It was Mr. Langenau. I
started up and exclaimed, "Mr. Langenau, how impru-
dent! Oh, go back at once."

He seemed weak, and his hand shook as he leaned

against the casement, but his eyes were glittering with a feverish excitement. He did not answer. I went on : " The Doctor forbade your coming out for several days yet—and the exertion and the night-air—oh, I beg you to go back."

"Alone?" he said in a low voice.

"No, oh no, I will go with you. Anything, only do not stay here a moment longer; come." And taking his hand (and how burning hot it was!) and drawing it through my arm, I started toward the hall. He had to lean on me, for the unusual exertion seemed to have annihilated all his strength. When we reached the library, I led him to a chair—a large and low and easy one, and he sank down in it.

"You are not going away?" he asked, as he gasped for breath, " For there is something that must be said to-night."

"No, I will not go," I answered, frightened to see him so, and agitated by a thousand feelings. "I will light the lamp, and read to you. Let me move your chair back from the window."

"No, you must not light the lamp; I like the moonlight better. Bring your chair and sit here by me—here." He leaned and half-pulled toward him the companion to the chair on which he sat, a low, soft, easy one.

I sat down in it, sitting so I nearly faced him. The moon was shining in at the one wide window: I can remember exactly the pattern that the vine-leaves made as the moonlight fell through them on the carpet at our feet. I had a bunch of verbena-leaves fastened in my dress, and I never smell verbena-leaves at any time or place without seeing before me that moon-traced pattern and that wide-open window.

"Pauline," he said, in that low, thrilling voice, leaning a little toward me, "I have a great deal to say to you to-night. I have a great wrong to ask pardon for—a great sorrow to tell you of. I shall never call you Pauline again as I call you to-night. I shall never look into your eyes again, I shall never touch your hand. For we must part, Pauline; and this hour, which heaven has given me, is the last that we shall spend together on the earth."

I truly thought that his fever had produced delirium, and, trying to conceal my alarm, I said, with an attempt to quiet him, " Oh, do not say such things; we shall see each other a great, great many times, I hope, and have many more hours together."

" No, Pauline, you do not know so well as I of what I speak. This is no delirium; would to heaven it were, and I might wake up from it. No, the parting must be said to-night, and I must be the one to speak it. We may spend days, perhaps, under the same roof—we may even sit at the same table once again; but, I repeat, from this day I may never look into your eyes again, I may never touch your hand. Pauline, can you forgive me? I know that you can love. Merciful Heaven! who so well as I, who have held your stainless heart in my stained hand these many dreamy weeks; and Justice has not struck me dead. Yes, Pauline, I know you've loved me; but remember this one thing, in all your bitter thoughts of me hereafter: remember this, you have not loved me as I have loved you. You have not given up earth and heaven both for me as I have done for you. For you? No, not for you, but for the shadow of you, for the thought of you, for these short weeks of you. And then, an eternity of absence, and of remorse, and of oblivion—ah, if it might be oblivion for you! If I could blot out of your life this short, blighting summer; if I could put you back to where you were that fresh, sweet morning that I walked with you beside the river! I loved you from that day, Pauline, and I drugged my conscience, and refused to heed that I was doing you a wrong in teaching you to love me. Pauline, I have to tell you a sad story: you will have to go back with me very far; you will have to hear of sins of which you never dreamed in your dear innocence. I would spare you if I could, but you must know, for you must forgive me. And when you have heard, you may cease to love, but I think you will forgive. Listen."

Why should I repeat that terrible disclosure? why harrow my soul with going back over that dark path? Let me try to forget that such sins, such wrongs, such revenges, ever stained a human life. I was so young, so innocent, so ignorant. It was a strange misfortune that I should have had to know that which aged and changed me so. But he was right in saying that I had to know it. My life was bound involuntarily to his by my love, and what concerned him was my fate. Alas! He was in no other way bound to me than by my love: nor ever could be.

I don't know whether I was prepared for it or not: I knew that something terrible and final was to come, and I felt the awe that attends the thoughts that words are final and time limited. But when I heard the fatal truth—that another woman lived to whom he was irrevocably bound—I heard it as in a dream, and did not move or speak. I think I felt for a moment as if I were dead, as if I had passed out of the ranks of the living into the abodes of the silent, and benumbed, and pulseless. There was such a horrible awe, and chill, and check through all my young and rapid blood. It was like death by freezing. It is not so pleasant as they say, believe me. But no pain: that came afterward, when I came to life, when I felt the touch of his hand on mine, and ceased to hear his cruel words.

I had shrunk back from him in my chair, and sat, I suppose, like a person in a trance, with my hands in my lap, and my eyes fixed on him with bewilderment. But when he ceased to speak—and, leaning forward on one knee, clasped my hands in his, and drew me toward him, then indeed I knew I was not dead. Oh, the agony of those few moments—I tried to rise, to go away from him. But he held me with such strength—all his weakness was gone now. He folded his arms around my waist and held me as in a vise. Then suddenly leaning his head down upon my arms, he kissed my hands, my arms, my dress, with a moan of bitter anguish.

"Not mine," he murmured. "Never mine but in my dreams. O wretched dreams, that drive me mad. Pauline, they will tell us that we must not dream— we must not weep, we must be stocks and stones. We must wear this weight of living death till that good Lord that makes such laws shall send us death in mercy. Twenty, thirty, forty, fifty years of suffering: that might almost satisfy Him, one would think.

Pauline! you and I are to say good-bye to-night. Good-bye! People talk of it as a cruel word. Think of it: if it were but for a year, a year with hope at the end of it to keep our hearts alive, it would be terrible, and we should need be brave. The tears that lovers shed over a year apart; the days that have got to come and go, how weary. The nights—the nights that sleep flies off from, and that memory reigns over. Count them—over three hundred come in every year. One, you think while it is passing, is enough to kill you: one such night of restless torture, and how many shall we multiply our three hundred by? We are young, Pauline. You are a child, a very child. I am in the very flush and strength of manhood. There is half a century of suffering in me yet: this frame, this brain, will stand the wear of the hard years to come but too, too well. There is no hope of death. There is no hope in life. That star has set. Good God! And that makes hell—why should I wait for it—it cannot be worse there than here. Don't listen to me—it will not be as hard for you—you are so young—you have no sins to torture you—only a little love to conquer and forget. You will marry a man who lives for you, and who is patient and will wait till this is over. Ah, no: by Heaven! I can't quite stand it yet. Pauline, you never loved him, did you

—never blushed for him—never listened for his coming with your lips apart and your heart fluttering, as I have seen you listen when you thought that I was coming? No, I know you never loved him: I know you have loved me alone—me—who ought to have forbidden you. Forgive—forgive—forgive me."

A passion of tears had come to my relief, and I shook from head to foot with sobs. I cannot feel ashamed when I remember that he held me for one moment in his arms. He had been to me till that shock, strength, truth, justice: *the man I loved.* How could I in one instant know him by his sin alone, and undo all my trust? I knew only this, that it was for the last time, and that my heart was broken.

I forgave him—that was an idle form; in my great love I never felt that there was anything to be forgiven, except the wrong that fate had done me, in making my love so hopeless. He told me to forget him; that seemed to me as idle; but all his words were precious, and all my soul was in his hand. When, at that moment, the sound of wheels upon the gravel came, and the sound of laughter and of voices, I sprang up; he caught me in his arms and held me closely. Another moment, the parting was over, and I was kneeling by my bed up-stairs, weeping, sobbing, hopeless.

CHAPTER XIII.

THE WORLD GOES ON THE SAME.

Into my chamber brightly
  Came the early sun's good-morrow;
On my restless bed, unsightly,
  I sat up in my sorrow.

Faust.

It is an amazing thing, the strength and power of
pride. Pride, and the law of self-respect and self-
preservation in our being, is the force that holds us
in our course. When we reflect upon it, how few of
all the myriads fly out from it and are lost. That I
ate my meals; that I dressed myself with care; that
I took walks and drives: that I did not avoid my
companions, and listened patiently to what they chose
to say: these were the evidences of that centripetal
law within that was keeping me from destruction. It
would be difficult to imagine a person more unhappy.
Undisciplined and unfortified by the knowledge that
disappointment is an integral part of all lives, there
had suddenly come upon me a disappointment the
most total. It covered everything; there was not a
flicker of hope or palliation. And I had no idea

where to go to make myself another hope, or in what course lay palliation. As we have prepared ourselves or have been prepared, so is the issue of our temptations. My great temptation came upon me, foolish, ignorant, unprepared : the wonder would have been if I had resisted it to my own credit.

The days went on as usual at R——, and I must hold my place among the careless daughters and not let them see my trouble. Careless daughters, indeed they were, and I shuddered at the thought of their cold eyes : no doubt their eyes, bright as well as cold, saw that something was amiss with me; with all my bravery, I could not keep the signs of wretchedness out of my pale face. But they never knew the story, and they could only guess at what made me wretched. It is amazing (again) what power there is in silence, and how much you can keep in your hands if you do not open them. People may surmise—may invent, but they cannot know your secret unless you tell it to them, and their imaginings take so many forms, the multitude of things that they create blot out all definite design. Thus every one at R—— had a different theory about my loss of spirits and the relapse of Mr. Langenau, but no one ever knew what passed that night.

Richard came. He was closeted with Sophie until

8

after midnight, but I do not think he told her anything that she desired to know. I think he only tried
to find out from her what had passed (and she did not
know that I had been in the library since she spoke to
me). If Mr. Langenau had been well, I have no
doubt that it was his design to have dismissed him on
the following day, no matter at what hazard. How
much he knew I cannot tell, but enough to have warranted him in doing that, perhaps. He probably
would have put it in Mr. Langenau's power to have
gone without any coloring put upon his going that
would have affected his standing in the household.
This was his design, no doubt; otherwise he would
have told his sister all. His delicate consideration for
me made him guard as sacred the fact that I had
wasted my hope and love so cruelly.

He was not going away again, I soon found; *qui va
à la chasse perd sa place.* He had lost his place, but
he would stay and guard me all the same; and
the chase for gold seemed given up for good and
all.

Kilian was in constant surprise, and made out many
catechisms, but he got little satisfaction.

Richard was going to have a few weeks' "rest,"
unless something should occur to call him back to
town.

He sought no interview with me, was kind and silent, but his eye was never off me. I think he watched his opportunity for saying what he had to say to Mr. Langenau, but such an opportunity seemed destined not to come.

Mr. Langenau was ill the day after Richard came home—quite ill enough to cause alarm. He had a high fever, and the Doctor even seemed uneasy, and prescribed the profoundest quiet. After a day or two, however, he improved, and all danger seemed averted.

As soon as he was strong enough, he was to be removed to his own room above, for the sake of quiet, and to release the household from its enforced tranquillity.

All these particulars I heard at table, or from morning groups on the piazza: with stony cheeks, and eyes that looked unflinchingly into all curious faces: so works the law of self-defence.

All but Richard, I am sure, were staggered, but he read with his heart.

I never blushed now, I never faltered, I never said a word I did not mean to say. It was a struggle for life: though I did not value the life, and should have found it hard to say why

I did not give up and let them see that I was killed.

But I kept wondering how I should sustain myself if I should be called upon to meet him once again.

CHAPTER XIV.

GUARDED.

Forever at her side, and yet forever lonely,
I shall unto the end have made life's journey, only
Daring to ask for naught, and having naught received.
Felix Arvers.

Duty to God is duty to her; I think
God, who created her, will save her too
Some new way, by one miracle the more
Without me. Then, prayer may avail, perhaps.
R. Browning.

"Mr. LANGENAU is coming down to-day," said Charlotte Benson in a stage-whisper, as we took our places at the table, a week after this. "I met him in the hall about an hour ago, looking like a ghost, and he told me he was coming down to dinner."

"*Vraiment,*" said Sophie, looking a little disconcerted. "Well, he shall have Charley's place. Charley isn't coming."

"I hope he's in a better temper than that last day we saw him," said Henrietta.

"Poor fellow!" said Charlotte, "that was the day before the fever began. It was coming on: that was the reason of it all, no doubt. He looks ghastly enough now. You'll forgive all, the moment that you see him."

Charlotte had forgiven him herself, though she had never resumed the rôle of Florence Nightingale. Since he had given up the library and removed to his own room, he had been quite lost to all, and nobody seemed to have gone near him, not even Sophie, who would have been glad to forget that he existed, without doubt.

Richard's eyes were on me as Charlotte said "Hush!" and a step crossed the hall in the pause that ensued. Kilian, sitting next me, began to talk to me at that moment, the moment that Mr. Langenau entered the room. And I think I answered quite coherently: though two sets of words were going through my brain, the answer to his commonplace question, and the words that Mr. Langenau had said that night, "Pauline, I shall never look into your eyes again, I shall never touch your hand."

It seemed to me an even chance which sentence saw the day; but as the walls did not fall down about me and no face looked amazement, I found I must have answered Kilian's question with propriety.

There were many voices speaking at once; but there was such a ringing in my ears, I could not distinguish who spoke, or what was said: for a moment

I was lost, if any one had taken advantage of it. But gradually I regained my senses: one after another they each took up their guard again: and I looked up. And met his eyes? No; but let mine rest upon his face. And then I found I had not measured my temptation, and that there was something to do besides defending myself from others' eyes. For there was to defend myself from my own heart. The passion of pity and tenderness that rushed over me as my eyes fell on his haggard face, so strong and yet so wan, swept away for the moment the defences against the public gaze. I could have fallen down at his feet before them all and told him that I loved him.

A few moments more of the sound of commonplace words, and the repulsion of every-day faces and expressions, swept me back into the circle of conventionalities, and brought me under the force of that current that keeps us from high tragedy.

All during the meal Mr. Langenau was grave and silent, speaking little and then with effort. He had overrated his strength, perhaps, for he went away before the end of the dinner, asking to be excused, in a tone almost inaudible. After he had gone, a good many commentaries were offered. Kilian seemed to express the sense of the assembly when he said:

" The man looks shockingly, and he's not out of the woods yet."

Sophie looked troubled: she had some compunctions for the neglect of the last few days, perhaps.

" What does the Doctor say ?" pursued her brother.

" Nothing, I suppose—for he hasn't been here for a week, almost."

" Well, then, you'd better send for him, if you don't want the fellow to die on your hands. He's not fit to be out of bed, and you'll have trouble if you don't look out."

" As if I hadn't had trouble," returned his sister, almost peevishly.

" Well, I beg your pardon, Sophie. But I fancied you and Miss Charlotte were in charge ; and I thought about ten days ago, your patient was in a fair way to be killed with kindness, and it's a little of a surprise to me to find he's being let alone so very systematically."

" Why, to tell you the truth," cried Charlotte Benson, " we were turned out of office without much ceremony, one fine day after dinner. I am quite willing to be forgiving; but I don't think you can ask me to put myself in the way of being snubbed again to that extent."

" The ungrateful varlet ! what did he complain of ? Hadn't he been coddled enough to please him ? Did he want four or five more women dancing attendance on him ?"

"Oh, it was not want of attention he complained of. In fact," said Charlotte, coloring, "It was that he didn't like quite so much, and wanted to be allowed more liberty."

Kilian indulged in a good laugh, which wasn't quite fair, considering Charlotte's candor.

"But the truth is," said Charlotte, uneasily, "that he was too ill, that day, to be responsible for what he said. He was just coming down with the fever, and, you know, people are always most unreasonable then."

"I'm very glad I never gave him a chance to dispense with me," said Mary Leighton, with a view to making herself amiable in Kilian's eyes.

"I think he dispensed with you early in the season," said Charlotte, sharply. "Oh, hast thou forgotten that walk that he took, upon your invitation? Ah, Miss Leighton, his look was quite dramatic. I know you never have forgiven him."

"I haven't the least idea what you are talking of," returned Mary Leighton, with bewildered and child-like simplicity.

"Ah, then it was not as unique an occurrence as I hoped," said Charlotte, viciously. "I imagined it would make more of an impression."

8*

"Charlotte," interrupted Sophie, shocked at this open impoliteness, "I hope you are forgiving enough to break it to him that he's got to see the Doctor; for if he comes unexpectedly and goes up to his room, he will be dramatic, and that is so unpleasant, as we know to our sorrow."

"Indeed, I shan't tell him," cried Charlotte, "you can take your life in your hand, and try it if you please; but I cannot consent to risk myself. There's Mary Leighton, she bears no malice. Perhaps she'll go with you as support."

"Ha, ha!" cried Kilian. "Richard, you and I may be called on to bring up the rear. There's the General's old sword in the hall, and I'll take the Joe Manton from the shelf in the library."

"Richard looks as if he disapproved of us all very much," said Sophie, and in truth Richard did look just so. He did not even answer these suggestions, but began after a moment to talk to Henrietta on indifferent matters.

It was on this afternoon that a new policy was inaugurated at R——. We were taught to feel that we had been quite aggrieved by the dullness of the past two weeks or more, and that we must be compensated by some refreshing novelties.

Richard was at the head of the movement—Richard

with his sober cares and weary look. But the incongruity struck no one; they were too glad to be amused. Even Sophie brightened up. Charlotte was ready to throw her energies into any active scheme, hospital or picnic, charity-school or kettle-drum.

"To-morrow will be just the sort of day for it," said Richard, "cool and fine. And half the pleasure of a picnic is not having time to get tired of it beforehand."

"That's very true," said Charlotte; "but I don't see how we're going to get everybody notified and everything in order for nine o'clock to-morrow morning."

"Nothing easier," said Kilian; "we'll go, directly after tea, to the De Witts and Prentices, and send Thomas with a note to the Lowders. Sophie has done her part in shorter time than that, very often; and I don't believe we should be starved, if she only gave half an hour's notice to the cook."

What is heavier than pleasure-seeking in which one has no pleasure? I shall never forget the misery of those plans and that bustle. I dared not absent myself, and I could scarcely carry out my part for very heavy-heartedness. It seemed to me that I could not bear it, if the hour came, and I should have to drive away with all that merry party, and leave poor Mr. Langenau for a long, long day alone.

I felt sure something would occur to release me: it could not be that I should have to go. With the exaggeration of youth, it seemed to me an impossibility that I could endure anything so grievous. How I hated all the careless, thoughtless, happy household! Only Richard, enemy as he was to my happiness, seemed endurable to me. For Richard was not merry-making in his heart, and I was sure he was sorry for me all the time he was trying to oppose me.

Mr. Langenau was again in the Doctor's care, who came that evening, and who said to Richard, in my hearing, he must be kept quiet; he didn't altogether like his symptoms.

Richard had his hands full, with great matters and small. Sophie had washed hers of the invalid; there had been some sharpish words between the sister and brother on the matter, I imagine, and the result was, Richard was the only one who did or would do anything for his comfort and safety.

That day, after appearing at dinner, he came no more. I watched with feverish anxiety every step, every sound; but he came not. I knew that the Doctor's admonitions would not have much weight, nor yet Richard's opinion. I had the feeling that if he would only speak to me, only look at me once, it would ease that horrible oppression and pain which I was suffering. The agony I was enduring was so intolerable, and its real relief so impossible, like a child I caught at some fancied palliation, and craved only that. What would one look, one word be—out of a lifetime of silence and separation.

No matter: it was what I raged and died for, just one look, just one word more. He had said he would never look into my eyes again : that haunted me and made me superstitious. I would *make* him look at me. I would seize his hand and kneel before him, and tell him I should die if he did not speak to me once more. Once more! Just once, out of years, out of forever. I had thrown duty, conscience, thought to the winds. I had but one fear—that we should be finally separated without that word spoken, that look exchanged. I said to myself again and again, I shall die, if I cannot speak to him again. Beyond that I did not look. What better I should be after that speaking I did not care. I only longed and looked for that as a relief from the insufferable agony of my fate. One cannot take in infinite wretchedness : it is our nature to make dates and periods to our sorrows in our imagination.

And so that horrid afternoon and evening passed, amid the racket and babel of visitors and visiting. I followed almost blindly, and did as the others did.

The next morning dawned bright and cold. What a day for summer! The sun was brilliant, but the wind came from over icebergs; it seemed like "winter painted green."

We were to start at nine o'clock. I was ready early, waiting on the piazza for the aid to fate that was to keep me from the punishment of going. No human being had spoken his name that morning. How should I know whether he were still so ill or no.

The hour for starting had arrived. Richard, who never kept long out of sight of me, was busy loading the wagon that was to accompany us, with baskets of things to eat, and with wines and fruits. Kilian was engrossed in arranging the seats and cushions in the two carriages which had just driven to the door.

Mary Leighton was fluttering about the flower-bed at the left of the piazza, making herself lovely with geranium and roses. Sophie, in a beautiful costume, was pacifying Charley, who had had a difference with his uncle Kilian. Charlotte and Henrietta were busy in their small way over a little basket of preserves; and two or three of the neighboring gentlemen, who were to drive with us, were approaching the house by a side-entrance.

In a moment or two we should be ready to be off. What should I do? I was frantic with the thought that he might be worse, he might go away. I was to be absent such a length of time. I must—I would see him before we went. What better moment than the present, when everybody was engaged in this fretting, foolish picnic. I would run up-stairs—call to him outside his door—make him speak to me.

With a guilty look around, I started up, stole through the group on the piazza, and ran to the stairs. But alas, Richard had not failed to mark my movements, and before my foot had touched the stair his voice recalled me. I started with a guilty look, and trembled, but dared not meet his eye.

"Pauline, are you going away? We are just ready start."

If I had had any presence of mind I should have made an excuse, and gone to my own room for a moment, and taken my chance of getting to the floor above ; but I suppose he would have forestalled me. I could not command a single word, but turned back and followed him. As we got into the carriage, the voices and the laughing really seemed to madden me. Driving away from the house, I never shall forget the sensation of growing heaviness at my heart ; it seemed to be turning into lead. I glanced back at the closed windows of his room and wondered if he saw us, and if he thought that I was happy.

The length of that day! The glare of that sun! The chill of that unnatural wind! Every moment seemed to me an hour. I can remember with such distinctness the whole day, each thing as it happened; conversations which seemed so senseless, preparations which seemed so endless. The taste of the things I tried to eat: the smell of the grass on which we sat, and the pine-trees above our heads: the sound of fire blazing under the teakettle, and the pained sensation of my eyes when the smoke blew across into our faces: the hateful vibration of Mary Leighton's laugh: all these things are unnaturally vivid to me at this day.

I don't know what the condition of my brain must have been, to have received such an exaggerated impression of unimportant things.

"What can I do for you, Miss Pauline?" said Kilian, throwing himself down on the grass at my feet. I could not sit down for very impatience, but was walking restlessly about, and was now standing for a moment by a great tree under which the table had been spread. It was four o'clock, and there was only vague talk of going home; the horses had not yet been brought up, the baskets were not a quarter packed. Every one was indolent, and a good deal tired; the gentlemen were smoking, and no one seemed in a hurry.

When Kilian said, "What can I do for you, Miss Pauline?" I could not help saying, "Take me home."

"Home!" cried Kilian. "Here is somebody talking about going home. Why, Miss Pauline, I am just beginning to enjoy myself! only look, it is but four o'clock."

"Oh, let us stay and go home by moonlight," cried Mary Leighton, in a little rapture.

"Would it not be heavenly!" said Henrietta.

"How about tea?" said Charlotte. "We shall be hungry before moonlight, and there isn't anything left to eat."

"How material!" cried Kilian, who had eaten an enormous dinner.

"We shall all get cold," said Sophie, who loved to be comfortable, "and the children are beginning to be very cross."

"Small blame to them," muttered a dissatisfied man in my ear, who had singled me out as a companion in discontent, and had pursued me with his contempt for pastoral entertainments, and for this entertainment in especial.

"Well, let the people that want to stay, stay; but let us go home," I said, hastily.

"That is so like you, Pauline," exclaimed Mary Leighton, in a voice that stung me like nettles.

"It is very like common-sense," I said, "if that's like me."

" Well, it isn't particularly."·

"Let dogs delight," said Kilian, "I have a compromise to offer. If we go home by the bridge we pass the little Brink hotel, where they give capital teas. We can stop there, rest, get tea, have a dance in the 'ball-room,' sixteen by twenty, and go home by moonlight, filling the souls of Miss Leighton and Henrietta with bliss."

A chorus of ecstasy followed this; Sophie herself was satisfied with the plan, and exulted in the prospect of washing her face, and lying down on a bed for half an hour, though only at a little country inn. Even this low form of civilized life was tempting, after seven hours spent in communion with nature on hard rocks.

Great alacrity was shown in getting ready and in getting off. I could not speak to any one, not even the dissatisfied man, but walked away by myself and tried to let no one see what I was feeling. After all was ready, I got into the carriage beside one of the Miss Lowders, and the dissatisfied man sat opposite. He wore canvas shoes and a corduroy suit, and sleeve-buttons and studs that were all bugs and bees. I think I could make a drawing of the sleeve-button on the arm with which he held the umbrella over us;

there were five different forms of insect-life repre-
sented on it, but I remember them all.

"I'm afraid you haven't enjoyed yourself very
much," said Miss Lowder, looking at me rather
critically.

"I? why—no, perhaps not; I don't generally enjoy
myself very much."

Somebody out on the front seat laughed very
shrilly at this: of course it was Mary Leighton, who
was sitting beside Kilian, who drove. I felt I would
have liked to push her over among the horses, and
drive on.

"Isn't her voice like a steel file?" I said with great
simplicity to my companions. The dissatisfied man,
writhing uncomfortably on his seat, four inches too
narrow for any one but a child of six, assented
gloomily. Miss Lowder, who was twenty-eight years
old and very well bred, looked disapproving, and
changed the subject. Not much more was said after
this. Miss Lowder had a neuralgic headache, developed by the cold wind and an undigested dinner eaten
irregularly. She was too polite to mention her sufferings, but leaned back in the carriage and was silent.

My vis-à-vis was at last relieved by the declining
sun from his task, and so the umbrella-arm and its
sleeve-button were removed from my range of vision.

We counted the mile-posts, and we looked sometimes at our watches, and so the time wore away.

Kilian and Mary Leighton were chattering incessantly, and did not pay much attention to us. Kilian
drove pretty fast almost all the way, but sometimes
forgot himself when Mary was too seductive, and let
the horses creep along like snails.

" There's our little tavern," cried Kilian at last,
starting up the horses.

" Oh, I'm so sorry," murmured Mary Leighton, " we
have had such a lovely drive."

My vis-à-vis groaned and looked at me as this
observation reached us. I laughed a little hysterically:
I was so glad to be at the half-way house—and Mary
Leighton's words were so absurd. When we got out
of the carriage, the dissatisfied man stretched his long
English limbs out, and lighting his cigar, began silently
to pace the bricks in front of the house.

Kilian took us into the little parlor (we were the
first to arrive), and committed us to the care of a thin,
tired-looking woman, and then went to see to the
comfort of his horses.

The tired woman, who looked as if she never had
sat down since she grew up, took us to some rooms,
where we were to rest till tea was ready. The rooms
had been shut up all day, and the sun had been beat-

ing on them: they smelled of paint and dust and ill-brushed carpets. The water in the pitchers was warm and not very clear: the towels were very small and thin, the beds were hard, and the pillows very small, like the towels: they felt soft and warm and limp, like sick kittens. We threw open the windows and aired the rooms, and washed our faces and hands : and Miss Lowder lay down on the bed and put her head on a pile of four of the little pillows collected from the different rooms. Mary Leighton spent the time in re-arranging her hair, and I walked up and down the hall, too impatient to rest myself in any way.

By-and-by the others came, and then there was a hubbub and a clatter, and poor Miss Lowder's head was overlooked in the mêlée; for these were all the rooms the house afforded for the entertainment of wayfarers, and as there were nine ladies in our party, it is not difficult to imagine the confusion that ensued.

Benny and Charley also came to have their hair arranged, and it devolved on Charlotte and me to do it, as their mamma had thrown herself exhausted on one of the beds, and with the bolsters doubled up under her head, was trying to get some rest.

It was fully half-past seven before the tea-bell rang. I seized Benny's hand, and we were the first on the ground. I don't know how I thought this would be useful in hurrying matters, for Benny's tea and mine were very soon taken, and were very insignificant fractions of the general business.

There were kerosene lamps on the table, and everything was served in the plainest manner, but the cooking was really good, and it was evident that the tired woman had been on her feet all her life to some purpose. Almost every one was hungry, and the contrast to the cold meats, and the hard rocks, and the disjointed apparatus of the noonday meal, was very favorable.

Richard had put me between himself and Benny, and he watched my undiminished supper with disapprobation : but I do not believe he ate much more himself. He put everything that he thought I might like, before me, silently : and I think the tired woman (who was waitress as well as cook), must have groaned over the frequent changing of my plate.

" Do not take any more of that," he said, as I put out my hand for another cup of coffee.

"Well, what shall I take ?" I exclaimed peevishly. But indeed I did not mean to be peevish, nor did I know quite what I said, I was so miserable. Richard sighed as he turned away and answered some question of Sophie ; who was quite revived.

Charlotte and Henrietta each had an admirer, one of the Lowders, and a young Frenchman who had come with the Lowders.

It had evidently been a very happy day with all the young ladies from the house. After tea the gentlemen must smoke, and after the smoking there was to be dancing. The preparations for the dancing created a good deal of amusement and consumed a great deal of time. Kilian and young Lowder went a mile and a half to get a man to play for them. When he came, he had to be instructed as to the style of music to be furnished, and the rasping and scraping of that miserable instrument put me beside myself with nervousness. Then the "ball-room" had to be aired and lighted; then the negro's music was found to be incompatible with modern movements; even a waltz was proved impossible, and nobody would consent to remember a quadrille but Richard. So they had to fall back upon Virginia reels, and everybody was made to dance.

The dissatisfied man was at my side when the order was given. He turned to me languidly, and offered me his hand.

"No," I exclaimed, biting my lips with impatience, and added, "You will excuse me, won't you?"

He said, with grave philosophy, "I really think it will seem shorter than if we were looking on."

I accepted this wise counsel, and went to dance with him. And what a dance it was! The blinking kerosene lamps at the sides of the room, the asparagus boughs overhead, the grinning negro on the little platform by the door: the amused faces looking in at the open windows: the romping, well-dressed, pretty women: the handsome men who were trying to act like clowns: the noise of laughing and the calling out of the figures: all this, I am sure, I never shall forget. And, strange to say, I somewhat enjoyed it after all. The coffee had stimulated me: the music was merry: I was reckless, and my companions were full of glee. Even the *ennuyé* skipped up and down the room like a school-boy: I never shall forget Richard's happy and relieved expression, when I laughed aloud at somebody's amusing blunder.

Then came the reaction, when the dancing was over, and we were getting ready to go home. It was a good deal after ten o'clock, and the night was cold. There were not quite shawls enough, no preparations having been made for staying out after dark. Richard went up to Sophie (I was standing out by the steps to be ready the moment the carriages should come), and I heard him negotiating with her for a shawl for me. She was quite impatient and peremptory, though *sotto voce.* The children needed both her extra ones, and there was an end of it.

I did not care at all, and feeling warm with dancing, did not dread what I had not yet felt. I pulled my light cloak around me, and only longed for the carriage to arrive. But after we had started and were about forty rods from the door, quite out of the light of the little tavern, just within a grove of locust-trees (the moon was under clouds), Richard's voice called out to Kilian to stop, and coming up to the side of the carriage, said, " Put this around you, Pauline, you haven't got enough." He put something around my shoulders which felt very warm and comfortable : I believe I said, Thank you, though I am not at all sure, and Kilian drove on rapidly.

By-and-by, when I began to feel a little chilly, I drew it together round my throat: the air was like November, and, August though it was, there was a white frost that night. I was frightened when I found what I had about my shoulders. It was Richard's coat. I called to Kilian to stop a moment, I wanted to speak to Richard. But when we stopped, the carriage in which he was to drive was just behind us—and some one in it said, Richard had walked. He had not come back after he ran out to speak to us—

must have struck across the fields and gone ahead.
And Richard walked home, five miles, that night!
the only way to save himself from the deadly chill of
the keen air, without his coat.

When we drove into the gate, at home, I stooped
eagerly forward to get a sight of the house through
the trees. There was a light burning in the room
over mine: that was all I wanted to know, and with
a sigh of relief I sank back.

When we went into the hall, I remembered to hang
Richard's coat upon a rack there, and then ran to my
room. I could not get any news of Mr. Langenau,
and could not hear how the day had gone with him:
could only take the hope that the sight of the little
lamp conveyed.

CHAPTER XV.

Go on, go on :
Thou canst not speak too much; I have deserved
All tongues to talk their bitterest.

Winter's Tale.

OF course, the night was entirely sleepless after such a day. I was over-tired, and the coffee would have been fatal to rest in any case. I tossed about restlessly till three o'clock, and then fell into a heavy sleep.

The sun was shining into the room, and I heard the voices of people on the lawn when I awoke. When I went down, after a hurried and nervous half-hour of dressing, I found the morning, apparently, half gone, and the breakfast-table cleared.

Mary Leighton, with a croquet mallet in her hand, was following Kilian through the hall to get a drink of water. She made a great outcry at me and my appearance.

"What a headache you must have," she cried. "But ah! think what you've missed, dear! The tutor has been down at breakfast, or rather at the breakfast-table, for he didn't eat a thing. He is a little paler than he was at dinner day before yesterday—and he's gone up-stairs; and we've voted that we hope he'll stay there, for he depresses us just to look at him."

And then, with an unmeaning laugh, she tripped on after Kilian to get that drink of water, which was nothing but a ticket for a moment's *tête-à-tête* away from the croquet party. Richard had seen me by this time, and came in and asked how I felt, and rang the bell in the dining-room, and ordered my breakfast brought. He did not exactly stay and watch it, but he came in and out of the dining-room enough times to see that I had everything that was dainty and nice (and to see, alas! that I could not eat it); for that piece of news from Mary Leighton had levelled me with the ground again.

That I had missed seeing him was too cruel, and that he looked so ill; how could I bear it?

After my breakfast was taken away, I went into the hall, and sat down on the sofa between the parlor doors. Pretty soon the people came in from the croquet ground, talking fiercely about a game in which Kilian and Mary had been cheating. Charlotte Benson was quite angry, and Charley, who had played with her, was enraged. I thought they were such fools to care, and Richard looked as if he thought they were all silly children. The day was warm and close, such a contrast to the day before. The sudden cold had broken down into a sultry August atmosphere. The sun, which had been bright an hour ago, was becoming obscured, and the sky was grayish. Every one felt languid. We were all sitting about the hall, idly, when a servant brought a note. It was an invitation; that roused them all—and for to-day. There was no time to lose.

The Lowders had sent to ask us all to a croquet party there at four o'clock.

" What an hour !" cried Sophie, who was tired ; " I should think they might have let us get rested from the picnic."

But Charlotte and Henrietta were so much charmed at the prospect of seeing so soon the Frenchman and the young devoted Lowder, that they listened to no criticism on the hour or day.

" How nice !" they said, " we shall get there a little before five—play for a couple of hours—then have tea on the lawn, perhaps—a little dance, and home by moonlight." It was a ravishing prospect for their unemployed imaginations, and they left no time in rendering their answer.

For myself, I had taken a firm resolve. I would

never repeat the misery of yesterday; nothing should persuade me to go with them, but I would manage it so that I should be free from every one, even Richard.

Croquet parties are great occasions for pretty costumes; all this was talked over. What should I wear? Oh, my gray grenadine, with the violet trimmings, and a gray hat with violet velvet and feather.

"You have everything so perfect for that suit," said Mary Leighton, in a tone of envy. "Cravat and parasol and gloves of just the shade of violet."

"And gray boots," I said. "It *is* a pretty suit." No one but Sophie had such expensive clothes as I, but I cannot say at that moment they made me very happy. I was only thinking how improbable that the gray suit would come out of the box that day, unless I should be obliged to dress to mislead the others till the last.

The carriages (for we filled two), were to be at the door at four o'clock punctually. The Lowders were five miles away: the whole thing was so talked about and planned about, that when dinner was over, I felt we had had a croquet party, and quite a long one at that.

Mr. Langenau did not come to dinner; Sophie sent a servant to his room after we were at table, to ask

him if he would come down, or have his dinner sent
to him; but the servant came back, saying he did
not want any dinner, with his compliments to Mrs.
Hollenbeck.

"*À la bonne heure,*" cried Kilian. "A skeleton
always interferes with my appetite at a feast."

"It is the only thing, then, that does, isn't it?"
asked Charlotte, who seemed to have a pick at him
always.

"No, not the only thing. There is one other—just
one other."

"And, for the sake of science, what is that?"

"A woman with a sharp tongue, Miss Charlotte.—
Sophie, I don't think much of these last soups. Your
famous cook's degenerating, take my word."

And so on, while Charlotte colored, and was silent
through the meal. She knew her tongue was sharp;
she knew that she was self-willed and was not humble.
But she had not taken herself in hand, religiously; to
take one's self in hand morally, or on grounds of ex-
pediency, never amounts to much; and such taking
in hand was all that Charlotte had as yet attempted.
In a little passion of self-reproach and mortification,
she occasionally lopped off ugly shoots; but the root
was still vigorous and lusty, and only grew the better
for its petty pruning. Richard looked very much

displeased at his brother's rudeness, and tried to make up for it by great kindness and attention.

About this time I had become aware of what were Sophie's plans for Richard. In case he must marry (to be cured of me), he was to marry Charlotte, who was so capable, so sensible, of so good family, so much indebted to Sophie, and so decidedly averse to living in the country. Sophie saw herself still mistress here, with, to be sure, a shortened income, and Richard and his wife spending a few weeks with her in the summer. I do not know how far Charlotte entered into these plans. Probably not at all, consciously; but I became aware that, as a little girl, Richard had been her hero; and he did not seem to have been displaced by any one entirely yet. But I took a very faint interest in all this. I should have cared, probably, if I had seen Richard devoted to her. He seemed to belong to me, and I should have resented any interference with my rights. But I did not dread any. I knew, though I took little pleasure in the knowledge, that he loved me with all his good and manly heart; and it never seemed a possibility that he could change.

The simple selfishness of young women in these matters is appalling. Richard was mine by right of conquest, and I owed him no gratitude for the service of his life. That other was the lord who had the right inalienable over me. I bent myself in the dust before him. I would have taken shame itself as an honor from his hands. I thought of him day and night. I filled my soul with passionate admiration for his good deeds, his ill deeds, his all. And the other was as the ground beneath my feet, of which I seldom thought.

Richard met me at the foot of the stairs, after dinner, as I was going up.

" Pauline, will you go in the carriage with Charlotte and Sophie ? I am going to drive."

" Oh, it doesn't make any difference," I answered, with confusion. " Anywhere you choose."

I think he had misgivings about my going from that moment ; to allay which, I called out something about my costume to Sophie as I went up to my room. The day was growing duller, and stiller, and grayer. I sat by the window and watched the leaden river. It was like an afternoon in September, before the chill of the autumn has come. Not a leaf moved upon the trees, not a cloud crept over the sky. It was all one dim, gray, gloomy stillness overhead. I wondered if they would have rain. *They*, not I, for I was going to stay at home, and before they came back I should have seen him. I said that over and over to myself

9*

with bated breath, and cheeks that burned like flame. Every step that passed my door made me start guiltily. Once, when some one knocked, I pulled out my gray dress, and flung it on the bed, before I answered.

It was approaching four o'clock. I undressed myself rapidly, put on a dressing-sack, and threw myself upon the bed. What should I say when they came for me? They could not *make* me go. I felt very brave. At last the carriages drove up to the door. I crept to the window to see if any one was ready. While I was watching through the half-closed blinds, some one crossed the piazza. My heart gave a great leap, and then every pulse stood still. It was Mr. Langenau. His step was slower than it used to be, and, I thought, a little faltering. He crossed the road, and took the path that led through the grove and garden to the river. He had a book under his arm; he must be going to the boat-house to sit there and read. My heart gave such an ecstasy of life to my veins at the thought, that for a moment I felt sick and faint, as I drew back from the window.

I threw myself on the bed as some one knocked. It was a servant to tell me they were ready. I sent word to Mrs. Hollenbeck that I was not well, and should not be able to go with them. Then I lay still and waited in much trepidation for the second knock.

I heard in a few moments the rustle of Sophie's dress outside. She was not pleased at all. She could scarcely be polite. But then everything looked very plausible. There lay my dress upon the bed, as if I had begun to dress, and I was pale and trembling, and I am sure must have looked ill enough to have convinced her that I spoke the truth.

She made some feeble offer to stay and take care of me. "Oh, pray don't," I cried, too eagerly, I am afraid. And then she said her maid should come and stay with me, for the children were going with them, and there would be nothing for her to do. I stammered thanks, and then she went away. I did not dare to move till after I had heard both carriages drive off, and all voices die away in the distance.

Bettina came to the door, and was sent away with thanks. Then I began to dress myself with very trembling hands. This was new work to me, this horrible deception. But all remorse for that, was swallowed up in the one engrossing thought and desire which had usurped my soul for the days just passed.

It was a full half-hour before I was ready, my hands shook so unaccountably, and I could scarcely find the things I wanted to put on. When I went to the door I could hardly turn the key, I felt so weak, and

I stood in the passage many minutes before I dared go on. If any one had appeared or spoken to me, I am quite sure I should have fainted, my nerves were in such a shaken state.

CHAPTER XVI.

> Were Death so unlike Sleep,
> Caught this way? Death's to fear from flame, or steel,
> Or poison doubtless; but from water—feel!
>
> *Robert Browning.*

I MET no one in the hall or on the piazza. The house was silent and deserted: one of the maids was closing the parlor windows. She did not look at me with any surprise, for she had not probably heard that I was ill.

Once in the open air I felt stronger. I took the river-path, and walked quickly, feeling freed from a nightmare: and my mind was filled with one thought. "In a few moments I shall be beside him, I shall make him look at me, he cannot help but touch my hand." I did not think of past or future, only of the greedy, passionate present. My infatuation was at its height. I cannot imagine a passion more absorbing, more unresisted, and more dangerous. I passed quickly through the garden without even noticing the flowers that brushed against my dress.

As I reached the grove I thought for one instant of the morning that he had met me here, just where the paths intersected. At that moment I heard a step; and full of that hope, with a quick thrill, I glanced in the direction of the sound. There, not ten yards from me, coming from the opposite direction, was Richard. I felt a shock of disappointment, then fear, then anger. What right had he to dog me so? He looked at me without surprise, but as if his heart was full of bitterness and sorrow. He approached, and turned as if to walk with me.

"I want to be alone," I said angrily, moving away from him.

"No, Pauline," he answered with a sigh, as he turned from me, "you do not want to be alone."

Full of shame and anger, and jarred with the shock and fear, I went on more slowly. The wood was so silent—the river through the trees lay so still and leaden. If it had not been for the fire burning in my heart, I could have thought the world was dead.

There was not a sound but my own steps; should I soon meet him, would he be sitting in his old seat by the boat-house door, or would he be wandering along the dead, still river-bank? What should I say to him? O! he would speak. If he saw me he would have to speak.

I soon forgot that I had met Richard, that I had been angry; and again I had but this one thought.

The pine cones were slippery under my feet. I held by the old trees as I went down the bank, step by step. I had to turn and pass a clump of trees before I reached the boat-house door.

I was there! With a beating heart I stepped up on the threshold. There were two doors, one that opened on the path, one that opened on the river. The house was empty. I had a little sinking pang of disappointment, but I passed on to the door looking out on the river. By this door was a seat, empty, but on this lay a book and a straw hat. I could feel the hot blushes cover my face, my neck, as I caught sight of these. I stooped down, feeling guilty, and took up the book. It was a book which he had read daily to me in our lesson-hours. It had his name on the blank page, and was full of his pencil-marks. I meant to ask him to give me this book; I would rather have it than anything the world held, when I should be parted from him. *When!* I sat down on the seat beside the door, with the book lying in my lap, the straw hat on the bench. I longed to take it in my hands—to wreathe it with the clematis that grew about the door, as I had done one foolish, happy afternoon, not three weeks ago. But with a strange inconsistency, I dared not touch it; my face grew hot with blushes as I thought of it.

How should I meet him? Now that the moment I had longed for had arrived, I wondered that I had dared to long for it. I felt that if I heard his step, I should fly and hide myself from him. The recollection of that last interview in the library—which I had lived over and over, nights and days, incessantly, since then, came back with fresh force, fresh vehemence. But no step approached me, all was silent; it began to impress me strangely, and I looked about me. I don't know at what moment it was, my eye fell upon the trace of footsteps on the bank, and then on the mark of the boat dragged along the sand; a little below the boat-house it had been pushed off into the water.

I started to my feet, and ran down to the water's edge (at the boat-house the trees had been in the way of my seeing the river any distance).

I stood still, the water lapping faintly on the sand at my feet; it was hardly a sound. I looked out on the unruffled lead-colored river: there, about quarter of a mile from the bank, the boat was lying: empty —motionless. The oars were floating a few rods from her, drifting slowly, slowly, down the stream.

The sight seemed to turn my warm blood and

blushes into ice: even before I had a distinct impression of what I feared, I was benumbed. But it did not take many moments for the truth, or a dread of it, to reach my brain.

I covered my eyes with my hands, then sprang up the bank and called wildly.

My voice was like a madwoman's, and it must have sounded far on that still air. In less than a moment Richard came hurrying with great strides down the path. I sprang to him, and caught his arm and dragged him to the water's edge.

"Look," I whispered—pointing to the hat and book —and then out to the boat. I read his face in terror. It grew slowly, deadly white.

"My God!" he said in a tone of awe. Then shaking me from him, sprang up the bank, and his voice was something fearful as he shouted, as he ran, for help.

There were men laboring, two or three fields off. I don't know how long it took them to get to him, nor how long to get a boat out on the water, nor what boat it was. I know they had ropes and poles, and that they were talking in eager, hurried voices, as they passed me.

I sat on the steps that led down the bank, clinging to the low railing with my hands: I had sunk down because my strength had given way all at once, and I felt as if everything were rocking and surging under me. Sometimes everything was black before me, and then again I could see plainly the wide expanse of the river, the wide expanse of the gray sky, and between them—the empty, motionless boat, and the floating oars beyond upon the tide.

The voices of the men, and the splashing of the water, when at last they were launched and pulling away from shore, made a ringing, frightful noise in my head. I watched till I saw them reach the boat —till I saw one of them get over in it. Then while they groped about with ropes and poles, and lashed their boats together, and leaned over and gazed down into the water, I watched in a strange, be-numbed state.

But, by-and-by, there were some exclamations—a stir, and effort of strength. I saw them pulling in the ropes with combined movement. I saw them leaning over the side of the boat, nearest the shore, and together trying to lift something heavy over into it. I saw the water dripping as they raised it—and then I think I must have swooned. For I knew nothing further till I heard Richard's voice, and, raising my head, saw him leaping from the boat upon the bank. The other boat was further out, and was approaching slowly. I stood up as he came to me, and held by the railing.

"I want you to go up to the house," he said, gently, "there can be no good in your staying here."

"I will stay," I cried, everything coming back to me. "I will—will see him."

"There is no hope, Pauline," he said, in a quick voice, for the boat was very near the bank, "or very little—and you must not stay. Everything shall be done that can be done. I will do all. But you must not stay."

"I will," I said, frantically, trying to burst past him. He caught my arms and turned me toward the boat-house, and led me through it, out into the path that went up to the grove.

"Go home," he said, in a voice I never shall forget. "You shall not make a spectacle for these men. I have promised you I will do all. Mind you obey me strictly, and go up to your room and wait there till I come."

I don't know how I got there. I believe Bettina found me at the entrance to the garden, and helped me to the house, and put me on my bed.

An hour passed—perhaps more—and such an hour! (for I was not for a moment unconscious, after this, only deadly faint and weak), and then Richard came.

The door was a little open, and he pushed it back and came in, and stood beside the bed.

I suppose the sight of me, so broken and spoiled by suffering, overcame him, for he stooped down suddenly, and kissed me, and then did not speak for a moment.

At last he said, in a voice not quite steady, " I didn't mean to be hard on you, Pauline. But you know I had to do it."

"And there isn't any—any—" I gasped for the words, and could hardly speak.

" No, none, Pauline," he said, keeping my hand in his. " The doctors have just gone away. It was all no use."

" Tell me about it," I whispered.

"About what?" he said, looking troubled.

"About how it happened."

"Nobody can tell," he answered, averting his face. "We can only conjecture about some things. Don't try to think about it. Try to rest."

"How does he look?" I whispered, clinging to his hand.

"Just the same as ever; more quiet, perhaps," he answered, looking troubled.

I gave a sort of gasp, but did not cry. I think he was frightened, for he said, uneasily,

"Let me call Bettina; she can give you something— she can sit beside you."

I shook my head, and said, faintly, "Don't let her come."

"I have sent for Sophie," he said, soothingly. "She will soon be here, and will know what to do for you."

"Keep her out of this room," I cried, half raising myself, and then falling back from sudden faintness. "Don't let her come *near* me," I panted, after a moment, "nor any of them, but, most of all, Sophie; remember—don't let her even look at me;" and with moaning, I turned my face down on the pillow. I had taken in about a thousandth fraction of my great ca lamity by that time. Every moment was giving to me some additional possession of it.

Some one at that instant called Richard, in that subdued tone that people use about a house in which there is one dead.

"I have got to go," he said, uneasily. I still kept hold of his hand. "But I will come back before very long; and I will tell Bettina to bring a chair and sit outside your door, and not let any one come in."

"That will do," I said, letting go his hand, "only I don't want my door shut tight."

I felt as if the separation were not so entire, so tremendous, while I could hear what was going on below, and know that no door was shut between us—no door! Bettina, in a moment more, had taken up her station in the passage-way outside.

I heard people coming and going quietly through the hall below. I heard doors softly shut and opened.

I knew, by some intuition, that *he* was lying in the library. They moved furniture with a smothered sound; and when I heard two or three men sent off on messages by Richard, even the horses' hoofs seemed to be muffled as they struck the ground. This was the effect of the coming in of death into busy, household life. I had never been under the roof with it before.

About dusk a servant came to the door, with a tray of tea and something to eat, that Mr. Richard had sent her with.

"No," I said, "don't leave it here."

But, in a few moments, Richard himself brought it back. I can well imagine how anxious and unhappy he felt. He had, perhaps, never before had charge of any one ill or in trouble, and this was a strange experience.

"You must eat something, Pauline," he said. "I want you to. Sit up, and take this tea."

I was not inclined to dispute his will, but raised my

head, and drank the tea, and ate a few mouthfuls of the biscuit. But that made me too ill, and I put the plate away from me.

"I am very sorry," I said, meekly, "but I can't eat it. I feel as if it choked me."

He seemed touched with my submissiveness, and, giving Bettina the tray, stood looking down at me as if he did not know how to say something that was in his mind. Suddenly my ear, always quick, now exaggeratedly so, caught sound of carriage-wheels. I started up and cried, "They are coming," and hid my face in my hands.

"Don't be troubled," he said, "you shall not be disturbed."

"Oh, Richard," I exclaimed, as he was going away, after another undecided movement as if to speak, "you know what I want."

"Yes, I know," he said, in a low voice.

"And now they're come, I cannot. They will see him, and I cannot."

"Be patient. I will arrange for you to go. Don't, don't, Pauline."

For I was in a sort of spasm, though no tears came, and my sobs were more like the gasps of a person being suffocated, than like one in grief.

"If you will only be quiet, I will take you down,

after a few hours, when they are all gone to their rooms. Pauline, you'll kill me ; don't do so—Pauline, they'll hear you. Try not to do so; that's right—lie down and try to quiet yourself, poor child. I can't bear to go away ; but there is Sophie on the stairs."

He had scarcely time to reach the hall before Sophie burst upon him with almost a shriek.

"What is this horrible affair, Richard? What a terrible disgrace and scandal! we never shall get over it. Will it get in the papers, do you think? I am so ill—I have been in such a state since the news came. Such a drive home as this has been! Oh, Richard, tell me all about it quickly. Where is Pauline? how does she bear it?" making for my door.

Richard put out his hand and stopped her. I had sprung up from the bed, and stood, trembling violently, at the further extremity of the room. I do not know what I meant to do if she came in, for I was almost beside myself at that moment.

She was persistent, angry, agitated. How well I knew the curiosity that made her so intent to gain admission to me. It was not so much that I dreaded being a spectacle, as the horror and hatred I felt at being approached by her coldness and hypocrisy, while I was so sore and wounded. I was hardly responsible; I don't think I could have borne the touch of her hand.

But Richard saved me, and sent her away angry. I crept back to the bed, and lay down on it again. I heard the others whispering as they passed through the hall. Mary Leighton was crying; Charlotte was silent. I don't think I heard her voice at all.

After a long while I heard them go down, and go into the dining-room. They spoke in very subdued tones, and there was only the slightest movement of china and silver, to indicate that a meal was going on. But this seemed to give me a more frantic sense of change than anything else. I flung myself across the bed, and another of those dreadful, tearless spasms seized me. Everything—all life—was going on just the same; even in this very house they were eating and drinking as they ate and drank before—the very people who had talked with him this day; the very table at which he had sat this morning. Oh! they were so heartless and selfish : every one was; life itself was. I did not know where to turn for comfort. I had a feeling of dreading every one, of shrinking away from every one.

"Oh!" I said to myself, "if Richard is with them at the table, I never want to see him again."

But Richard was not with them. In a moment or two he came to the door, only to ask me if I wanted anything, and to say he would come back by-and-by.

10

There was a question which I longed so frantically to ask him, but which I dared not; my life seemed to hang on the answer. *When were they going to take him away?* I had heard something about trains and carriages, and I had a wild dread that it was soon to be.

I went to the door and called Richard back, and made him understand what I wanted to know. He looked troubled, and said in a low tone,

"At four o'clock we go from here to meet the earliest train. I have telegraphed his friends, and have had an answer. I am going down myself, and it is all arranged in the best way, I think. Go and lie down now, Pauline; I will come and take you down soon as the house is quiet."

Richard went away unconscious of the stab his news had given me. I had not counted on anything so sudden as this parting. While he was in the house, while I was again to look upon his face, the end had not come; there was a sort of hope, though only a hope of suffering, something to look forward to, before black monotony began its endless day.

CHAPTER XVII.

BESIDE HIM ONCE AGAIN.

There are blind ways provided, the foredone
Heart-weary player in this pageant world
Drops out by, letting the main masque defile
By the conspicuous portal.

R. Browning.

What is this world? What asken men to have?
Now with his love—now in his cold grave—
Alone, withouten any companie!

Chaucer.

The tall old clock, which stood by the dining-room door, had struck two, and been silent many minutes, before Richard came to me. I had spent those dreadful hours in feverish restlessness : my room seemed suffocating to me. I had walked about, had put away my trinkets, I had changed my dress, and put on a white one which I had worn in the morning, and had tried to braid my hair.

The quieting of the house, it seemed, would never come. It was twelve o'clock before any one came upstairs. I heard one door after another shut, and then sat waiting and wondering why Richard did not come, till the moments seemed to grow to centuries. At last I heard him at the door, and I went toward it trembling, and followed him into the hall. He carried a light, for up-stairs it was all dark, and when we reached the stairway, he took my hand to lead me. I was trembling very much ; the hall below was dimly lit by a large lamp which had been turned low. Our steps on the bare staircase made so much noise, though we tried to move so silently. It was weird and awful. I clung to Richard's hand in silence. He led me across the hall, and stopped before the library-door. He let go my hand, and taking a key from his pocket, put it in the lock, turned it slowly, then opened the door a little way, and motioned me to enter.

Like one in a trance, I obeyed him, and went in alone. He shut the door noiselessly, and left me with the dead.

That was the great, the immense hour of my life. No vicissitude, no calamity of this mortal state, no experience that may be to come, can ever have the force, the magnitude of this. All feelings, but a child's feelings, were comparatively new to me, and here, at one moment, I had put into my hand the plummet that sounded hell; anguish, remorse, fear—a woman's heart in hopeless pain. For I will not believe that any child, that any woman, had ever loved more absolutely, more passionately, than I had loved the man who lay there dead before me. But I cannot talk about what I felt in those moments; all that concerns what I write is the external.

The—coffin was in the middle of the room, where the table ordinarily stood—where my chair had been that night, when he told me his story. Surely if I sinned, in thought, in word, *that* night, I paid its full atonement, *this.* Candles stood on a small table at the head of where he lay, and many flowers were about the room. The smell of verbena-leaves filled the air: a branch of them was in a vase that some one had put beside his coffin. The fresh, cool night-air came in from the large window, open at the top.

His face was, as Richard said, much as in life, only quieter. I do not know what length of time Richard left me there, but at last, I was recalled to the present, by his hand upon my shoulder, and his voice in a whisper, " Come with me now, Pauline."

I rose to my feet, hardly understanding what he said, but resisted when I did understand him.

" Come with me," he said, gently, " You shall come back again and say good-bye. Only come out into the hall and stay awhile with me; it is not good for you to be here so long."

He took my hand and led me out, shutting the door noiselessly. He took me across the hall, and into the parlor, where there was no light, except what came in from the hall. There was a sofa opposite the door, and to that he led me, standing himself before me, with his perplexed and careworn face. I was very silent for some time: all that awful time in the library, I had never made a sound: but suddenly, some thought came that reached the source of my tears, and I burst into a passion of weeping. I am not sure what it was: I think, perhaps, the sight of the piano, and the recollection of that magnificent voice that would never be heard again. Whatever it was, I bless it, for I think it saved my brain. I threw myself down upon the sofa, and clung to Richard's hand, and sobbed, and sobbed, and sobbed.

Poor fellow! my tears seemed to shake him terribly. Once he turned away, and drew his hand across his brow, as if it were a little more than he could bear. But some men, like many women, are born to sacrifice.

He tried to comfort and soothe me with broken words. But what was there to say?

"Oh, Richard," I cried, "What does it all mean? why am I so punished? was it so very wicked to have loved him after I knew all? Was all this allowed to come because I did that? Answer me, tell me; tell me what you think."

"No, Pauline, I don't think that was it. Don't talk about it now. Try to be quiet. You are not fit to think about it now."

"But, Richard, what else can it mean? I know, I know that it is the truth. God wouldn't have sent such a punishment upon me if he hadn't seen my sin."

"It's more likely He sent it to——" and then he paused.

I know now he meant, it was more likely He had sent it to save me from the sins of others; but he had the holy charity not to say it.

"Oh," I cried, passionately, "When all the sin was mine, that he should have had to die: when he never came near me, never looked at me: when he would rather die than break his word to me. That night in the library, after he had told me all, he said, 'I will never look into your eyes again, I will never touch your hand;' and though we were in the same room together after that, and in the same house all this time, and though he knew I loved him so—he never looked at me, he never turned his eyes upon me; and I—I was willing to sin for him—to die for him. I would have followed him to the ends of the earth, not twelve hours ago."

" Hush, Pauline," said Richard huskily, "you don't know what you're saying—you are a child."

" No, I'm not a child—after to-day, after to-night —I am not a child—and I know too well what I say —too well—too well. Richard, you don't know what has been in my heart. That night, he held me in his arms and kissed me—when he said good-bye. Then I was innocent, for I was dazed by grief and had not come to my senses, after what he told me. But to-day I said—*to-day*—to have his arms around me once again—to have him kiss me once again as he kissed me then—I would go away from all I ever had been taught of right and duty, and would be satisfied."

" Then, thank God for what has come," said Richard, hoarsely, wiping from his forehead the great drops that had broken out upon it.

" No!" I cried with a fresh burst of weeping. " No, I cannot thank God, for I want him back again. *I want him.* I had rather die than be separated from him. I cannot thank God for taking him away from me. Oh, Richard, what shall I do? I loved him, loved him so. Don't look so stern; don't turn away from me. You used to love me. Could you thank God for taking me away from you, out of your arms, warm, and strong, and living, and making me cold, and dumb, and stiff, like *that?*"

"Yes, Pauline, if it had been to save us both from sin."

"You don't know what love is, if you say that."

"I know what sin is, better than you do, maybe. Listen, Pauline. I've loved you ever since I saw you; men don't often love better than I have loved you; but I'd rather drag you, to-night, to that black river there, and hold you down with my own hands till the breath left your body, than see you turn into a sinful woman, and lead the life of shame you tell me you had it in your heart to lead, to-day."

"Is it so very awful?" I whispered with a shiver, my own emotion stilled before his. "I only loved him!"

"Forget you ever did," he said, rising, and pacing up and down the room.

I put my hands before my face, and felt as if I were alone in the world with sin. If this unspoken, passionate, sweet thought, that I had harbored, were so full of danger as to force God to blast me with such punishment, as to drive this tender, generous, loving man to wish me dead, what must be the blackness of the sin from which I had been saved, if I were saved? If there were, indeed, anything but shocks of woe and punishment, and deadly despair and darkness, in this strange world in which I found myself. There was a silence. I rose to my feet. I don't know what I meant to do or where to go ; my only impulse was to hide myself from the eyes of my companion, and to go away from him, as I had hidden myself from all others, since I was smitten with this chastisement.

"Forgive me, Pauline," he said, coming to my side. "It is the second time I have been harsh with you this dreadful day. This is what comes of selfishness. I hope you will forget what I have said."

I still turned to go away, feeling afraid of him and ashamed before him. He put out his hand to stop me.

"Pauline, remember, I have been sorely tried. I would do anything to comfort you. I haven't another wish in my heart but to be of use to you."

"Oh, Richard," I cried, bursting into tears afresh, and hiding my eyes, "if you give me up and drive me away from you, I am all alone. There isn't another human being that I love or that cares for me. Dear Richard, do be good to me ; do be sorry for me."

"I am sorry for you, Pauline ; you know that."

"And you will take care of me ?" I cried, stretching out my arms toward him, with a sudden overwhelming sense of my loneliness and destitution.

"Yes, Pauline, to the end of my life or of yours ; as if you were my sister or almost my child."

"Dear Richard," I whispered, as I buried my face on his arm, "if it were not for you I should not live through this dreadful time. I hope I shall die soon ; as soon as I am better. But till I do die, I hope you will be good to me, and love me." And I pressed his hand against my cheek and lips, like the poor, frantic, grief-bewildered child that I was.

At this moment there came a sound of movement in the stables : I heard one of the heavy doors thrown open, and a man leading a horse across the stable-floor. (The windows were open and the night was very still.) Richard started, and looked uneasily at his watch, stepping to the door to get the light.

"How late is it?" I faltered.

"Half-past three," he said, turning his eyes away, as if he could not bear the sight of my face. I do not like to remember the dreadful moments that followed this : the misery that I put upon Richard by my passionate, ungoverned grief. I threw myself upon the floor, I clung to his knees, I prayed him to delay the hour of going—another hour, another day. I said all the wild and frantic things that were in my heart, as he closed the library-door and led me to my room.

" Try to say your prayers, Pauline," was all he could answer me.

I did try to say them, as I knelt by the window, and saw in the dull, gray dawn, those two carriages drive slowly from the door.

Richard went away alone. Kilian indeed came down-stairs just as he was starting.

Sophie had awakened, and called him into her room for a few moments.

Then he came down, and I saw him get into the carriage alone, and motion the man to drive on, after that other—which stood waiting a few rods farther on.

CHAPTER XVIII.

He, full of modesty and truth,
Loved much, hoped little, and desired nought.
                                        Tasso.

Fresh grief can occupy itself
  With its own recent smart;
It feeds itself on outward things,
  And not on its own heart.
                        Faber

A THING which surprises me very much in looking over those days of suffering, is, that during that day a frightful irritability is the emotion that I most remember—an irritability of feeling, not of expression : for I lay quite still upon the bed all day, and only answered, briefly and simply, the questions of Sophie and the maid.

I could not sleep: it was many hours since I had slept: but nothing seemed further from possibility than sleeping. The lightest sound enraged my nerves : the approach of any one made me frantic. I lay with my hands crushed together, and my teeth against each other, whenever Sophie entered the room.

She tried to be sympathetic and kind: but she was not much encouraged. Toward afternoon, she left me a good deal alone. "I wonder how people feel when they are going mad," I said, getting up and putting cold water on my head. I was so engaged with the strange sensations that pursued me, that I did not dwell upon my trouble.

"Is this the way you feel when you are going to die? or what happens if you never go to sleep?" My body was so young and healthy, that it was making a good fight.

Just at dusk, Richard returned. In a little while, about half an hour, Sophie came and told me Richard would like to see me in her little dressing-room.

The day of panic and horror was over, and proprieties must begin their sway. I felt I hated Sophie for making me go out of my own room, but I pulled a shawl over my shoulders and followed her across the hall into her little room. There Richard was waiting for me. He gave me a chair, and then said, "You needn't wait, Sophie," and sat down beside me.

Sophie went away half angry, and Richard looked at me uneasily.

"I thought you'd want to see me," he said.

"Yes," I answered; "I wish you'd tell me everything," but in so commonplace a voice, I know that he was startled.

" You do not feel well, do you? Maybe we'd better not talk about it now."

" Oh, yes. You might as well tell me all to-night."

" Well, everything is done. The two persons to whom I telegraphed met me at the station. There was very little delay. I went with them to the cemetery."

" I am very glad of that. I thought perhaps you wouldn't go. Was there a clergyman, or don't they have a clergyman when—when—"

" There was a clergyman," said Richard, briefly.

" I hope you'll take me there some time," I said dreamily. " Should you know where to go—exactly?"

" Exactly," he answered. " But, Pauline, I am afraid you havn't rested at all to-day. Have you slept?"

" No; and I wish I could; my head feels so strangely—light, you know—and as if I couldn't think."

" Haven't you seen the Doctor?"

" No—and that's what I want to say. I *won't* have the Doctor here; and I want you to take me home to-morrow morning, early. I have put a good many of my clothes into my trunk, and Bettina will help

me with the rest to-night. Isn't there **any** train before the five o'clock?"

"No," said Richard, uneasily. "Pauline, I think
you'd better not arrange to go away to-morrow."

"If you don't take me out of this house I shall go
mad. I have been thinking about it all day, and I
know I shall."

Richard was silent for a moment, then, with the
wise instinct of affection, wonderful in man, and in a
man who had had no experience in dealing with
diseased or suffering minds, he acquiesced in my plan
to go ; told me that we would take the earliest train,
and interested me in thoughts about my packing.
About nine o'clock he came to my room-door, and I
heard some one with him. It was the Doctor.

I turned upon Richard a fierce look, and said, very
quietly, he . might go away, for I would not see the
Doctor. After that, they tried me with Sophie, but
with less success; and, finally, Richard came back
alone, with a glass in his hand.

"Take this, Pauline, it will make you sleep."

I wanted to sleep very much, so I took it.

Bettina had finished my packing, and had laid my
travelling dress and hat upon a chair.

"Shall Bettina come and sleep on the floor, by your
bed?" asked Richard, anxiously.

"No, I would not have her for the world."

"Maybe you might not wake in time," said Richard, warily.

That was very true : so I let Bettina come. Richard gave her some instructions at the door, and she came in and arranged things for the night, and lay down on a mattress at the foot of my bed.

The sedative which the Doctor sent did not work very well. I had very little sleep, and that full of such hideous, freezing dreams, that every time I woke, I found Bettina standing by my bed, looking at me with alarm. I had been screaming and moaning, she said. The screaming and moaning and sleeping (such as it was), were all over in about two hours, and then I had the rest of the night to endure, with the same strange, light feeling in my head—the restlessness not much, but somewhat abated.

I was very glad that Bettina was in the room, for though she was sleepy, and always a little stupid, she was human, and I was a coward, both in the matter of loneliness and of suffering. I made her sit by me, and take hold of my hand, and I asked her several times if she had ever been with any one that died, or that—I did not quite dare to ask her about going mad.

My questions seemed to trouble her. She crossed

herself, and shuddered, and said, No, she had never been with any one that died, and she prayed the good God never to let her be.

"You'll have to be with one person that dies, Bettina. That's yourself. You know it's got to come. We've all got to go out at that gate," and I moaned, and turned my face away.

"Let me call Mr. Richard," said Bettina, very much afraid. I would have given all the world to have seen Richard then; but I knew it was impossible, and I said, No, it would soon be morning.

Long before morning, I heard Richard up and walking about the house. We were to leave the house at half-past four. By four, all the trunks, and shawls, and packages, were strapped and ready, and I was sitting dressed, and waiting by the window.

Bettina liked very much better to pack trunks, and put rooms in order, than to sit still and hold a person's hot hands, in the middle of the night, and have dreadful questions asked her; and she had been very active and efficient. Soon Richard called her to come down and take my breakfast up to me. I could not eat it, and it was taken away. Then the carriage came, and the wagon to take the baggage. Finally, Richard came, and told me it was time to start, if I were ready.

Sophie came into the room in a wrapper, looking very dutiful and patient, and said all that was dutiful and civil. But I suppose I was a fiery trial to her, and she wished, no doubt, that she had never seen me, or better, that Richard never had. All this I felt, through her decently framed good-bye, but I did not care at all; to be out of her sight as soon as possible, was all that I requested.

When we went down in the hall, Richard looked anxiously at me, but I did not feel as if I had ever been there before; I really had no feeling. I said good-bye to Bettina, who was the only servant that I saw, and Richard put me into the carriage. When we drove away, I did not even look back. As we passed out of the gate, I said to him, "What day of the month is it to-day?"

"It is the first of September," he returned.

"And when did I come here?" I asked.

"Early in June, was it not?" he said. "You know I was not here."

"Then it is not three months," and I leaned back wearily in the carriage, and was silent.

Before we reached the city, Richard had good reason to think that I was very ill. He made me as comfortable as he could, poor fellow! but I was so restless, I could not keep in one position two minutes

at a time.   Several times I turned to him and said,
"It is suffocating in this car; cannot the window be
put up?" and when it was put up, I would seem to
feel no relief, and in a few moments, perhaps, would
be shaking with a nervous chill.   It must have been
a miserable journey, as I remember it.   Once I
said to Richard, after some useless trouble I had put
him to, "I am very sorry, Richard, I don't know how
to help it, I feel so dreadfully."

Richard tried to answer, but his voice was husky,
and he bent his head down to arrange the bundle of
shawls beneath my feet.   I knew that there were
tears in his eyes, and that that was the reason that he
did not speak.   It made me strangely, momentarily
grateful.

"How strange that you should be so good," I said
dreamily, "when Sophie is so hateful, and Kilian is
so trifling.   I think your mother must have been a
good woman."

I had never talked about Richard's mother before,
never even thought whether he had had one or not,
in my supreme and light-hearted selfishness.   But the
mind, at such a point as I was then, makes strange
plunges out of its own orbit.

"And she died when you were little?"

"Yes, when I was scarcely twelve years old."

"A woman ought to be very good when it makes so much difference to her children. Richard, did my uncle ever tell you anything about my mother—what sort of a woman she was, and whether I am like her?"

"He never said a great deal to me about it," Richard answered, not looking at me as he talked. "He thinks you are like her, very strikingly, I believe."

"Think! I haven't even a scrap of a picture of her, and no one has ever talked to me about her. All I have are some old yellow letters to my father, written before I was born. I think she loved my father very much. The noise of these cars makes me feel so strangely. Can't we go into the one behind? I am sure it cannot be so bad."

"This is the best car on the train, Pauline. I know the noise is very bad, but try to bear it for a little while. We shall soon be there." And so on, through the weary journey.

At one station Richard got out, and I saw him speaking to several men. I believe he was hoping to find a doctor, for he was thoroughly frightened.

Before we reached the city I was past being frightened for myself, for I was suffering too much to think of what might be the result of my condition. When we left the cars, and Richard put me in a carriage, the motion of the carriage and its jarring over the stones were almost unendurable. Richard was too anxious now to say much to me. The expression of relief on his face as we reached Varick-street was unspeakable. He hurried up the steps and rang the bell, then came back for me, and half carried me up the steps.

The door was opened by Ann Coddle, who was thrown into a helpless state of amazement by seeing me, not knowing why in this condition I did come, or why I came at all. She shrieked, and ejaculated, and backed almost down the basement stairs. Richard sternly told her she was acting like a fool, and ordered her to show him where Miss Pauline's room was, that he might take her to it.

" But her room isn't ready," ejaculated Ann, coming to herself, which was a wretched thing to come to, as poor Richard found.

" Not ready? well, make it ready, then. Go before me and open the windows, and I will put her on the sofa till you have the bed ready for her."

" The sofa—oh, Mr. Richard, it's all full of her dear clothes that have come up from the wash."

" Well, then, take them off—idiot—and do as you are told."

" Oh, Miss Pauline—oh, my poor, dear lamb. Oh, I'm all in a flutter; I don't know what to do. I'd better call the cook."

"Well, call the cook, then," said Richard, groaning, "only tell her to be quick."

All this time Richard was supporting me up the stairs. As we reached the top, Richard called out, "Tell Peter I want him at once, to take a message for me."

Ann was watching our progress up the stairs, with groans and ejaculations, forgetting that she was to call the cook. At the mention of Peter she exclaimed,

"He's laid up with the rheumatism, Mr. Richard. Oh, whatever shall we do!"

When we reached the middle of the second pair of stairs, I was almost helpless; Richard took me in his arms, and carried me.

"Is it this door, Pauline dear?" he said, opening the first he came to.

I should think the room had not been opened since I went away, it was so warm and close.

Richard carried me to the sofa, and scattered the *lingerie* far and wide as he laid me down upon it, and went to open the windows. Then he went to the bell and pulled it violently. In a few moments the cook came up (accompanied by Ann). She was a huge, unwieldy woman, but she had some intelligence, and knew better than to whimper.

"Miss Pauline is ill," he said, "and I want you to stay by her, and not leave her for a moment, till I come back. Make that woman get the room in order instantly, and keep everything as quiet as you can." To me: "I am going to bring a doctor, and I shall be back in a few moments. Do not worry, they will take good care of you."

When I heard Richard shut the carriage-door and drive away rapidly, I felt as if I were abandoned, and by the time he returned with the Doctor, I was in a state that warranted them in supposing me unconscious, tossing and moaning, and uttering inarticulate words.

The Doctor stood beside me, and talked about me to Richard with as much freedom as if I had been a corpse.

"I may as well be frank with you," he said, after a few moments of examination. "I apprehend great trouble from the brain. How long has she been in this condition?"

"She has been unlike herself since yesterday; as soon as I saw her, at seven o'clock last night, I noticed she was looking badly. She answered me in an abstracted, odd way, and was unlike herself, as I have said. But she had been under much excitement for some time."

"Tell me, if you please, all about it; and how long she has been under this excitement."

"She has been often agitated, and quite overstrained in feeling for some time. Three weeks ago I thought her looking badly. Two days ago she had a frightful shock—a suicide—which she was the first to discover. Since then I do not think that she has slept."

"Ah! poor young lady. She has had a terrible experience, and is paying for it. Now for what we can do for her. In the first place, who takes care of her?" with a look about the room.

"You may well ask. I have just brought her home, and find here, the man-servant ill, one woman too old and inactive to perform much service, and another to whom I would not trust her for a moment. I must ask *you*, who shall I get to take care of her?"

"You have no friend, no one to whom you could send in such a case? One of life and death,—I hope you understand?"

"None," answered Richard, with a groan. "There is not a person in the city to whom I could send for help. All my family—all our friends, are away. Is there no one that can be got for money—any money? no nurse that you could recommend?"

"I have a list of twenty. Yesterday I sent to every one, for a dangerous case of hemorrhage, and

11

could not find one disengaged.   It may be to-morrow
night before you get on the track of one that is at
liberty, if you hunt the city over.   And this girl is in
need of instant care ; her life hangs on it, you must
see."

"In God's name, then," said Richard, with a groan,
pacing up and down the room, "what am I to do ?"

"In *His* name, if you come to that," said the
Doctor, who was a good sort of man, notwithstanding
his professional cool ways, " there is a sisterhood, that
I am told offer to do things like this.   I never sent
to them, for I only heard of it a short time ago ; but
if you have no objection to crosses, and caps, and
ritualistic nonsense in its highest flower, I have no
doubt, that they will let you have a sister, and that
she'll do good service here."

" The direction," said Richard, too eager to be civil.
" How am I to get there ?"

The Doctor pulled over a pocket-case of loose
papers, and at last found one, which he handed his
companion.

" I give you three quarters of an hour to get back,"
he said. " I will stay here till then, at all events.   Do
not waste any time—nor spare any eloquence," he
added to himself, as Richard hurried from the room.

CHAPTER XIX.

Yes! it is well for us : from these alarms,
Like children scared, we fly into thine arms ;
And pressing sorrows put our pride to rout
With a swift faith which has not time to doubt.

Faber.

Learn by a mortal yearning to ascend
Towards a higher object.   Love was given,
Encouraged, sanctioned, chiefly for that end ;
For this the passion to excess was driven—
That self might be annulled ; her bondage prove
The fetters of a dream, opposed to love.

Wordsworth.

THE next thing that I recall, is rousing from slumber, or something related to slumber, and seeing a tall woman in the dress of a sister, standing by my bed. It was night, and there was a lamp upon a table near. The unusual dress, and the unfamiliarity of her whole appearance, made me start and stare at her, half raising myself in the bed.

"Why did you come here?" I said.   "Who sent for you?"

"I came because you were sick and suffering, and

I was sent in the Name ———" and bending her head slightly, she said a Name too sacred for these pages.

I gave a great sigh of relief, and sank back on my pillow. Her answer satisfied me, for I was not able to reason. I let her hold my hand; and all through that dark and troubled time submitted to her will, and desired her presence, and was soothed by her voice and touch.

Sister Madeline was not at all the ideal sister, being tall and dark, and with nothing peculiarly devotional or pensive in her cast of feature. Her face was a fine, earnest one. Her movements were full of energy and decision, though not quick or sharp. The whole impression left was that of one by nature far from humility, tenderness, devotion; but, by the force of a magnificent faith, made passionately humble, devout from the very heart, more than humanly compassionate and tender.

I never felt toward her as if she were "born so" —but as if she were rescued from the world by some great effort or experience; as if it were all "made ground," reclaimed from nature by infinite patience and incessant labor. She lived the life of an angel upon the earth. I never saw her, by look,

by word, or tone, transgress the least of the com-
mandments, so wonderful was the curb she held
over all her human feelings. Nor was this per-
fection attained by a sudden and grand sacrifice;
the consecration of herself to the religious life was
not the "single step 'twixt earth and heaven," but
it was attained by daily and hourly study—by the
practice of a hundred self-denials—by the most
accurate science of spiritual progress.

Doubtless, saints can be made in other ways, but
this is one way they can be made, starting with a
sincere intention to serve God. At least, so I believe, from knowing Sister Madeline.

She made a great change in my life, and I owe
her a great deal. It is not strange I feel enthusiasm
for her. I cannot bear to think what my coming
back to life would have been without her.

Of the alarming nature of my illness, I only
know that there were several days when Richard
never left the house, but waited, hour after hour, in
the library below, for the news of my condition,
and when even Uncle Leonard came home in the
middle of the day, and walked about the house,
silent and unapproachable.

One night—how well I remember it! I had been
convalescent, I do not know how long; I had passed

the childish state of interest in my *bouilli*, and
fretfulness about my *peignoir;* my mind had begun
to regain its ordinary power, and with the first efforts
of memory and thought had come fearful depression and despondency. I was so weak, physically,
that I could not fight against this in the least. Sister
Madeline came to my bedside, and found me in
an agony of weeping. It was not an easy matter
to gain my confidence, for I thought she knew nothing of me, and I was not equal to the mental effort
of explaining myself; she was only associated with
my illness. But at last she made me understand
that she was not ignorant of a great deal that
troubled me.

"Who has told you?" I said, my heart harden-
ing itself against Richard, who could have spoken
of my trouble to a stranger. .

"You, yourself," she answered me.

"I have raved?" I said.

"Yes."

"And who has heard me?"

"No one else. I sent every one else from the
room whenever your delirium became intelligible."

This made me grateful toward her; and I longed
for sympathy. I threw my arms about her and wept
bitterly.

"Then you know that I can never cry enough," I said.

"I do not know that," she answered. After a vain attempt to soothe me with general words of comfort, she said, with much wisdom, "Tell me exactly what thought gives you the most pain, now, at this moment."

"The thought of his dreadful act, and that by it he has lost his soul."

"We know with Whom all things are possible," she said, "and we do not know what cloud may have been over his reason at that moment. Would it comfort you to pray for him?"

"Ought I?" I asked, raising my head.

"I do not know any reason that you ought not," she returned. "Shall I say some prayers for him now?"

I grasped her hand: she took a little book from her pocket, and knelt down beside me, holding my hand in hers. Oh, the mercy, the relief of those prayers! They may not have done him any good, but they did me. The hopeless grief that was killing me, I "wept it from my heart" that hour.

"Promise me one thing," I whispered as she rose. "that you will read that prayer, every hour during the day, to-morrow, by my bed, whether I am sleeping or awake."

"I promise," she said, and I am sure she kept her word, that day and many others after it.

During my convalescence, which was slow, I had no other person near me, and wanted none. Uncle Leonard came in once a day, and spent a few minutes, much to his discomfort and my disadvantage. Richard I had not seen at all, and dreaded very much to meet. Ann Coddle fretted me, and was very little in the room.

Over these days there is a sort of peace. I was entering upon so much that was new and elevating, under the guidance of Sister Madeline, and was so entirely influenced by her, that I was brought out of my trouble wonderfully. Not out of it, of course, but from under its crushing weight. I know that I am rather easily influenced, and only too ready to follow those who have won my love. Therefore, I am in every way thankful that I came at such a time under the influence of a mind like that of Sister Madeline.

But the time was approaching for her to go away. I was well enough to do without her, and she had other duties. The sick-room peace and indulgence were over, and I must take up the burden of every-day life again. I was very unhappy, and felt as if I were without stay or guidance.

"To whom am I to go when I am in doubt?" I said; "you will be so far away."

"That is what I want to arrange: the next time you are able to go out, I want to take you to some one who can direct you much better than I."

"A priest?" I asked. "Tell me one thing: will he give me absolution?"

"I suppose he will, if he finds that you desire it."

"What would be the use of going to him for anything else?" I said. "It is the only thing that can give me any comfort."

"All people do not feel so, Pauline."

"But you feel so, dear Sister Madeline, do you not? You can understand how I am burdened, and how I long to have the bands undone?"

"Yes, Pauline, I can understand."

I am not inclined to give much weight to my own opinions, and as for my feelings, I know they were, then, those of a child, and in many ways will always be. I can only say what comforted me, and what I longed for. There had always been great force to me, in the Scripture that says, "Whosoever sins ye remit, they are remitted unto them, and whosoever sins ye retain, they are retained," even before I felt the burden of my sins.

I had once seen the ordination of a priest, and I sup-

11*

pose that added to the weight of the words ever after in my mind. I never had any doubt of the power then conferred, and I no sooner felt the guilt and stain of sin upon my soul, than I yearned to hear the pardon spoken, that Heaven offered to the penitent. I had been tangibly smitten ; I longed to be tangibly healed.

Whatever shame and pain there was about laying bare my soul before another, I gladly embraced it, as one poor means at my command of showing to Him whom I had offended, that my repentance was actual, that I stopped at no humiliation.

It may very well be that these feelings would find no place in larger, grander, more self-reliant natures ; that what healed my soul would only wound another. I am not prepared to think that one remedy is cure for all diseases, but I know what cured mine. I bless God for " the' soothing hand that Love on Conscience laid." I mark that hour as the beginning of a fresh and favored life ; the dawning of a hope that has not yet lost its power

> " to tame
> The haughty brow, to curb the unchastened eye,
> And shape to deeds of good each wavering aim."

CHAPTER XX.

THE HOUR OF DAWN.

Slowly light came, the thinnest dawn,
  Not sunshine, to my night;
A new, more spiritual thing,
  An advent of pure light.

All grief has its limits, all chastenings their pause;
Thy love and our weakness are sorrow's two laws.

THE winter that followed seemed very long and uneventful. After Sister Madeline went away, my days settled themselves into the routine in which they continued to revolve for many months. I was as lonely as formerly, save for the companionship of well-chosen books, and for the direction of another mind, which I felt to be the truest support and guidance. I was taught to bend to my uncle's wishes, and to give up constant church-going, and visiting among the poor, which would have been such a resource and occupation to me. And so my life, outwardly, was very little changed from former years—years that I had found almost insupportable, without any sorrow; and yet, strange to say, I was not unhappy.

My hours were full of little duties, little rules. (I

suppose my heart was in them, or I should have found them irksome.) Above all, I was not permitted to brood over the past: I was taught to feel that every thought of it indulged, was a sin, and to be accounted for as such: I could only remember the one for whom I mourned, on my knees, in my prayers. This checked, as nothing else could have done, the morbid tendency of grief, in a lonely, unoccupied, undisciplined mind. I was thoroughly obedient, and bent' myself with all simplicity to follow the instructions given me. Sometimes they seemed very irrelevant and useless, but I never rebelled against any, even one that seemed as hard to flesh and blood as this. And I have, sooner or later, seen the wisdom of them all, as I have worked out the problem of my correction.

Obedient as I was, though, and simple as the routine of my life continued, sometimes there came crises that were beyond my strength.

I can remember one; it was a furious storm—a day that nailed one in the house. There was something in the rage without that disturbed me; I wandered about the house, and found myself unable to settle to any task. Some one to speak to! Oh, it was so dreary to be alone. I went into my uncle's room where there were many books. Among those that were there I found one in French, (I have no idea

how it came there, I am sure my uncle had never read
it.) I carelessly turned it over, and finally became
absorbed in it. I came upon this passage:

"Quel plus noir abîme d'angoisse y a-t-il au
monde que le cœur d'un suicide? Quand le malheur d'un homme est dû à quelque circonstance de sa
vie, on peut espérer de l'en voir délivrer par un
changement qui peut survenir dans sa position.
Mais lorsque ce malheur a sa source en lui; quand
c'est l'âme elle-même qui est le tourment de l'âme;
la vie elle-même qui est le fardeau de la vie; que
faire, que de reconnaître en gémissant qu'il n'y a rien
à faire—rien, selon le monde; et qu'un tel homme,
plus à plaindre que ce prisonnier que l'histoire nous
peint dans les angoisses de la faim, se repaissant de
sa propre chair, est réduit à dévorer la substance
même de son âme dans les horreurs de son déses-
poir. Et qu'imagine-t-il donc pour échapper à lui-
même, comme à son plus cruel ennemi? Je ne dis
pas: 'Où ira-t-il loin de l'esprit de Dieu? où fuira-t-il
loin de sa face?' Je demande, où ira-t-il loin de son
propre esprit? où fuira-t-il loin de sa propre face?
Où descendra-t-il qu'il ne s'y suive lui-même; où se
cachera-t-il qu'il ne s'y trouve encore? Insensé,
dont la folie égale la misère, quand tu te seras tué, on
dira: 'Il est mort;' mais ce sont les autres qui le

diront; ce ne sera pas toi-même. Tu seras mort pour ton pays, mort pour ta ville, mort pour ta famille; mais pour toi-même, pour ce qui pense en toi, hélas! pour ce qui souffre en toi, tu vivras toujours.

Et comment ne sens-tu pas, que pour cesser d'être malheureux, ce n'est pas ta place qu'il faut changer, c'est ton cœur. Que tu disparaisses sous les flots, qu'un plomb meurtrier brise ta tête, ou qu'un poison subtil glace tes veines; quoi que tu fasses, et où que tu ailles, tu n'y peux aller qu'avec toi-même, qu'avec ton cœur, qu'avec ta misère! Que dis-je? Tu y vas avec un compte de plus à rendre, à la rencontre du grand Dieu qui doit te juger; tu y vas avec l'éternité de plus pour souffrir, et le temps de moins pour te repentir!

A moins que tu ne penses peut-être, parceque l'œil de l'homme n'a rien vu au-delà de la tombe, que cette vie n'ait pas de suite. Mais non, tu ne saurais le croire! Quand tous les autres le penseraient, toi, tu ne le pourrais pas. Tu as une preuve d'immortalité qui t'appartient en propre. Cette tristesse qui te consume, est quelque chose de trop intime et de trop profond pour se dissoudre avec tes organes, et ce qui est capable de tant souffrir ne peut pas s'aller perdre dans la terre. Les vers hériteront de la poussière de ton corps, mais l'amertume de ton âme, qui en héritera? Ces extases sublimes, ces tourments affreux; ces hauteurs des cieux, ces profondeurs des abîmes; qu'y a-t-il d'assez grand ou d'assez abaissé, d'assez élevé ou d'assez avili pour les revêtir en ta place? Non, tu ne saurais jamais croire que tout meurt avec le corps; ou si tu le pouvais tu 'n'en serais que plus insensé, plus misérable encore."

It is proof how child-like I had been, how obedient in suppressing all forbidden thoughts, that these words smote me with such horror. I had indulged in no speculation; I had never thought of him as haunted by the self he fled; as still bound to an inexorable and inextinguishable life,

> " With time and hope behind him cast,
> And all his work to do with palsied hands and cold."

The terrors I had had, had been vague. I had thought dimly of punishment, more keenly of separation. If I had analysed my thoughts, I suppose I should have found annihilation to have been my belief—death forever, loss eternal. But this—if this were truth—(and it smote me as the truth alone can smite), oh, it was maddening. To my knees! To my knees! Oh, that I might live long years to pray for him! Oh, that I might stretch out my hands to God for him, withered with age and shrunk with fasting, and strong but in faith and final perseverance! Oh, it could not be too late! What was prayer made for, but for a time like this? What was this little breath of time, compared with the Eternal Years, that we should only speak *now* for each other to our merciful God, and never speak for each other afterward? Spirits are forever; and is prayer only for the days of the body?

It was well for me that none of the doubts that are so often expressed had found any lodgment in my brain; if I had not believed that I had a right to pray for him, and that my prayers might help him, I cannot understand how I could have lived through those nights and days of thought.

CHAPTER XXI.

What to those who understand
Are to-day's enjoyments narrow,
Which to-morrow go again,
Which are shared with evil men,
And of which no man in his dying
Taketh aught for softer lying?

It was now early spring: the days were lengthen-
ing and were growing soft. Lent (late that year) was
nearly over. I had begun to think much about the
summer, and to wonder if I were to pass it in the
city. There was one thing that the winter had
developed in me, and that was, a sort of affection for
my uncle. I had learned that I owed him a duty,
and had tried to find ways of fulfilling it; had taken
a little interest in the house, and had tried to make
him more comfortable. Also I had prayed very constantly for him, and perhaps there is no way more
certain of establishing an affection, or at least a charity
for another, than that.

In return, he had been a little more human to me

than formerly, had shown some interest in my health, and continued appreciation of the fact that I was in the house. Once he had talked to me, for perhaps half an hour, about my mother, for which I was unspeakably grateful. Several times he had given me a good deal of money, which I had cared much less about. Latterly he had permitted me to go to church alone, which had seemed to me must be owing to Richard's intervention.

Richard had been almost as much as formerly at the house: my uncle was becoming more and more dependent on him. For myself, I did not see as much of him as the year before. We were always together at the table, of course. But the evenings that Richard was with my uncle, I thought it unnecessary for me to stay down-stairs. Besides, now, they almost always had writing or business affairs to occupy them.

It was natural that I should go away, and no one seemed to notice it. Richard still brought me books, still arranged things for me with my uncle (as in the matter of going to church alone), but we had no more talks together by ourselves, and he never asked me to go anywhere with him. At Christmas he sent me beautiful flowers, and a picture for my room. Sophie I rarely saw, and only longed never to see

Benny was permitted to come and spend a day with me, at great intervals, and I enjoyed him more than his mother or his uncle.

One day my uncle went down to his office in his usual health; at three o'clock he was brought home senseless, and only lived till midnight, dying without recovering speech or consciousness. It was a sudden seizure, but what everybody had expected; everybody was shocked for the moment, and then wondered that they were. It was very appalling to me; I was so unhappy, I almost believed I loved him, and I certainly mourned for him with simplicity and affection.

The preparations for the funeral were so frightful, and all the thoughts it brought so unnerving, that I was almost ill. A great deal came upon me, in trying to manage the wailing servants, and in helping Richard in arrangements.

It was the day after the funeral; I was tired out, and had lain down on the sofa in the dining-room, partly because I hated to be alone up-stairs, and partly because it was not far from lunch-time, and I felt too weary to take any needless steps. I don't think ever in my life before I had lain down on that sofa, or had spent two hours except, at the table, in that room. It was a most cheerless room, and no one ever thought of sitting down in it, except at meal-time. I closed the shutters and darkened it to suit my eyes, which ached, and I think must have fallen asleep.

The parlor was the room which adjoined the dining-room (only two large rooms on one floor, as they used to build), and separated from it by heavy mahogany columns and sliding-doors. These doors were half-way open, and I was roused by voices in the parlor. As soon as I recovered myself from the sudden waking, I recognized Sophie's and then Richard's. I wondered what Richard was doing up-town at that hour, and so Sophie did too, for she asked him very plainly.

" I thought I ought to come to see Pauline," she said, " but I did not suppose I should find you here in the middle of the day."

" There is something that I've got to see Pauline about at once," he said, " and so I was obliged to come up-town."

" Nothing has happened ? " she said interrogatively.

" No," he answered, evasively.

But she went on : " I suppose it's something in relation to the will; I hope she's well provided for, poor thing."

" Sophie," said her brother, with a change of tone,

"You'll have to hear it some time, and perhaps you may as well hear it now. It is that that I have come up-town about; there has been some strange mistake made; there is no will."

"No will!" echoed Sophie, "Why, you told me once —— "

"That he had left her everything. So he told me twice last year; so I have always believed to be the case. Since the day he died, the most faithful search has been made; there is not a corner of his office, of his library, of his room, that I have not hunted through. He was so methodical in business matters, so exact in the care of his papers, that I had little hope, after I had gone through his desk. I cannot understand it. It is altogether dark to me."

"What can have made him change his mind about it, Richard? Can he have heard anything about last summer?"

"Not from me, Sophie. But I have sometimes thought he knew, from allusions that he has made to her mother's marriage, more than once this winter."

"He was very angry about that, at the time, I suppose?"

"Yes, I imagine so. The man she married was poor, and a foreigner: two things he hated. I never heard there was anything against him but his poverty."

"How can he have heard about Mr. Langenau?" said Sophie, musingly.

"I think Pauline must have told him," said Richard.

"Pauline? never. She is much too clever; she never told him. You may be quite sure of *that.*"

"Pauline clever! Poor Pauline!" said Richard, with a short, sarcastic laugh, which had the effect of making Sophie angry.

"I am willing," she said, "that she should be as stupid and as good as you can wish ——. To whom does the money go?" she added, as if she had not patience for the other subject.

"To a brother, with whom he had a quarrel, and whom he had not seen for over sixteen years."

"Incredible!"

"But there had been some sort of a reconciliation, at least an exchange of letters, within these three months past."

"Ah!"

"And it is in consequence of hearing from him, and being pressed by his lawyer for an immediate settlement of the estate, that I have come up to tell Pauline, and to prepare her for her changed pros-pects."

"And what do you propose to advise?" asked Sophie, with a chilling voice.

"Heaven knows, Sophie," answered her brother, with a heavy sigh. "I see nothing ahead for the poor girl, but loneliness and trial. She is utterly unfit to struggle with the world. And she has not even a shelter for her head."

"Richard," interrupted his sister, with intensity of feeling in her voice, "I see what you are trying to persuade yourself: do not tell me, after what has passed, you still feel that you are bound to her—"

"*Bound!*" exclaimed Richard, with a vehemence most strange in him, as, pacing the room, he stood still before his sister. His back was toward me. She was so absorbed she did not see me as I darted past the folding-doors into the hall. As I flew panting up to my own room, I remember one feeling above all others, the first feeling of affection toward the house that I had ever had. It was mine no longer, my home never again; I had no right to stay in it a moment: my own room was not mine any more—the room where I had learned to pray, and to try to lead a good life—the room where I had lain when I was so near to death—the room where Sister Madeline had led me to such peaceful, quiet thoughts. I had but one wish now, not to see Richard, to escape Sophie, to get away forever from this house to which I had no right. I pulled down my hat and my street things, and dressed so quickly, that I had slipped down the stairs, and out into the street, before they had ceased · talking in the parlor. I heard their voices, very low, as I passed through the hall. I fully meant never to come back to the house again—not to be turned out.

My heart swelled as the door closed behind me. It was dreadful not to have a home. I was so unused to being in the street alone, that I felt frightened when I reached the cars and stopped them.

I was going to Sister Madeline. She would take me, and keep me, and teach me where to live, and how. I was a little confused, and got out at the wrong street, and had to walk several blocks before I reached the house.

The servant at the door met me with an answer that made me wonder whether there were anything else to happen to me on that day.

Sister Madeline had been called away—had gone on a long journey—something about the illness of her brother; and I must not come inside the door, for a contagious disease was raging, and the orders were strict that no one be admitted. I had walked so fast, and in such excitement of feeling, that I was weak and faint when I turned to go down the steps.

Where should I go? I walked on slowly now, and undecided, for I had no aim.

The clergyman to whom I had gone for direction in matters spiritual, was ill—for two weeks had given up even Lenten duties. Anything—but I could not go home, or rather where home had been. I walked and walked till I was almost fainting, and found myself in the Park. There the lovely indications of spring, and the quiet, and the fresh air, soothed me, and I sat down under some trees near the water, and rested myself. But the same giddy whirl of thoughts came back, the same incompetency to deal with such strange facts, and the same confusion. I do not know how long I wandered about; but I was faint and weary and hungry, and frightened too, for people were beginning to look at me.

It began to force itself upon me that I must go back to Varick-street after all, and take a fresh start. Then I began to think how I should get back, on which side must I go to find the cars—where was I, literally. Then I sat down to wait, till I should see some policeman, or some kind-looking person, near me, to whom I could apply for this very necessary information. In the meantime I took out my purse to see if I had the proper change. Verily, not that, nor any change at all! My heart actually stood still.

12

Yes, it was very true: I had given away, right and left, during this Lent: caring nothing for money, and being very sure of more when this was gone. I was literally penniless. I had not even the money to ride home in the cars.

Till a person has felt this sensation, he has not had one of the most remarkable experiences of life. To know where you can get money, to feel that there is some *dernier ressort,* however hateful to you, is one thing; but to *know* that you have not a cent—not a prospect of getting one—not a hope of earning one— no means of living—this is suffocation. This is the stopping of that breath that keeps the world alive.

The bench on which I happened to be sitting was one of those pretty, little, covered seats, which jut out into the lake. ˜I looked down into the water as I sat with my empty purse in my lap, and remembered vaguely the many narratives I had seen in the newspapers about unaccounted-for and unknown suicides. I could see how it might be inevitable—a sort of pressure, a fatality that might not be resisted. Even cowardice might be overcome when that pressure was put on.

It is a very amazing thing to feel that you have no money, nor any means of getting even eightpence: it chokes you: you feel as if the wheel had made its last revolution, and there was no power to make it turn again. It is not any question of pride, or of independence, when it comes suddenly ; it is a feeling of the inevitable ; you do not turn to others. You feel your individual failure, and you stand alone.

For myself, this was my reflection : I had not even a shelter for my head; Richard had said so. I had not a cent of money, and I had no means of earning any. The uncle who was coming to take possession of the house and furniture, was one whom I had been taught to distrust and dread. He would, perhaps, not even let me go into my room again, and would turn me out to-morrow, if he came : my clothes—were *they* even mine, or would they be given to me, if they were ? This uncle had reproached Uncle Leonard once for what he had done for me. I had even an idea that it was about my mother's marriage that the quarrel had occurred. And hard as I had regarded Uncle Leonard, he had been the soft-hearted one of the brothers, who had sheltered the little girl (after he had thrown off the mother, and broken her poor heart).

The house in Varick-street would be broken up. What would become of the cook, and Ann Coddle ? It would be easier for them to live than for me.

They could get work to do, for they knew how to

work, and people would employ them. I—I could do nothing, I had been taught to do nothing. I had never been directed how to hem a handkerchief. I had tried to dust my room one day, and the effort had tired me dreadfully, and did not look very well, as a result. I could not teach. I had been educated in a slipshod way, no one directing anything about it—just what it occurred to the person who had charge of me to put before me.

I had intended to throw myself upon Sister Madeline. But what then? What could she have done for me? I had asked her months before if I could not be a sister, and had been discouraged both by her and by my director. I believe they thought I was too young and too pretty, and, in fact, had no vocation. No doubt they thought I might soon look upon things differently, when my trouble was a little older.

And Richard—I did not give Richard many thoughts that day, for my heart was sore, when I remembered all his words. He had always thought that I was to be rich; perhaps that had made him so long patient with me. He had said I was not clever; he had seemed to be very sorry for me. He might well be. Sophie had asked him if he were still bound to me. I had not heard all his answer, but he had spoken in a tone of scorn. I did not want to think about him.

There was no whither to turn myself for help. And the clergyman, who had been more than kind to me, who had seemed to help me with words and counsel out of heaven,—he was cut off from my succor, and I stood alone—I, who was so dependent, so naturally timid, and so easily mistaken.

It was a dreary hour of my life, that hour that I sat looking over at the water of the pretty placid lake. I don't like to recall it. Some one passed by me, gave an exclamation of surprise, and came back hastily. It was Richard. He seemed so glad, and so relieved to see me—and to me it was like Heaven opening; notwithstanding my vindictive thoughts about him, I could have sprung into his arms; I felt protected, safe, the moment he was by me. I tried to speak, and then began to cry.

"I've been looking for you these last two hours," he said, sitting down beside me. "I came up-town to see you, and found you had gone out. I thought you would not be likely to go anywhere but to see Sister Madeline, and there the servant told me you had come this way. I could not find you here, and went back to Varick-street, then was frightened at hearing you had not come back, and returned again to look for you. What made you stay so long? Something has happened. Tell me what you are crying for."

I had no talent for acting, and not much discretion when I was excited; and he found out very soon that I knew what had befallen me. (I think he believed that Sophie had told me of it.)

"Were you very much surprised?" he said. "Had you supposed that you would be his heiress?"

"Why, no. I had not thought anything about it. I am afraid I have not thought much about anything this winter. I must have been very ungrateful, as well as childish, for I never have felt as if it were fortunate that I had a home, and as much money as I wanted. I did not care anything about being rich, you know—ever."

"No, I know you did not. I was sure you would have been satisfied with a very moderate provision."

"Oh, Richard," I cried, clasping my hands together, "if he had left me a little—just a little—just a few hundred dollars, when he had so much, to have kept me from having to work, when I don't know how to work, and am such a child."

"Work!" he exclaimed, looking down at me as if I were something so exquisite and so precious, that the very thought was profanation. "Work! no, Pauline, you shall not have to work."

"But what can I do?" I said, "I have nothing— and you know it; not a shelter; not the money to pay for my breakfast to-morrow morning. Not a person to whom I have a right to go for help; not a human being who is bound to care for me. Oh, I don't care what becomes of me; I wish that it were time for me to die."

Richard got up, and paced up and down the little platform with an absorbed look.

"It was so strange," I went on, "when he seemed . this winter to take a little notice of me, and to want to have me near him. I really almost thought he cared for me. And when I was so ill last Fall, don't you remember how often he used to come up to my room?"

"I remember—yes. It is all very strange."

"And some days early in the winter, when I could scarcely speak at table, I was so unhappy, he would look at me so long, and seem to think. And then would be very kind and gentle afterward, and do something to show he liked me—give me money, you know, as he always did." •

"Tell me, Pauline: did he ever ask you anything about last summer, or did you ever tell him?"

"No, Richard, I could never have spoken to him about it; and he never asked me. But I know he saw that I was not happy."

"Pauline," said Richard, after a pause, and as if forcing himself to speak, "there is no use in disguising from you what your position is: you know it yourself, enough of it, at least, to make you understand why I speak now. I don't know of any way out of it, but one; and I feel as if it were ungenerous to press that on you now, and, Heaven knows, I would not do it if I could think of anything else to offer to you. You know, Pauline, that if you will marry me, you will have everything that you need, as much as if your uncle had left you everything."

He did not look at me, but paced up and down the platform, and spoke with a thick, husky voice.

"You know it's been the object of my life, ever since I knew you, but I don't want that to influence you. I know it is too soon, a great deal too soon. And I would not have done it, if I could have seen anything else to do, or if you could have done without me."

I must have been deadly pale, for when at last he looked at me, he started.

"I don't know how it is," he said, with a groan, "I always have to give you pain, when, Heaven knows,

I'd give my life to spare you every suffering. I can't see any other way to take care of you than the way I tell you of, and yet, I have no doubt you think me cruel, and selfish, to ask you to do it now. It does seem so, and yet it is not. If you knew how much it has cost me to speak, you would believe it."

"I do believe it," I said, trying to command my voice. "I think you have always been too good and kind to me. But I can't tell you how this makes me feel. Oh, Richard, isn't there any, any other way ?"

"Perhaps there may be," he said, with a bitter and disappointed look, "but I do not know of it."

"Oh, Richard, do not be angry with me. Think how hard it is for me always to be disappointing you. I have a great deal of trouble !"

"Yes, Pauline, I know you have," he said, sitting down by me, and taking my hand in a repentant way. "You see I'm selfish, and only looked at my own disappointment just that minute. I thought I had not any hope that you might not mind the idea of marrying me; but you see, after all, I had. I believe I must have fancied that you were getting over your trouble: you have seemed so much brighter lately. But now I know the truth; and now I know that what I do is simply sacrifice and duty. A man must

12*

be a fool who looks for pleasure in marrying a woman who has no love for him. And I say now, in the face of it all, marry me, Pauline, if you can bring yourself to do it. I am the only approach to a friend that you have in the world. As your husband, I can care for you and protect you. You are young, your character is unformed, you are ignorant of the world. You have no home, no protection, literally none, and I am afraid to trust you. You need not be angry if I say so. I think I've earned the right to find some faults in you. I don't expect you to love me. I don't expect to be particularly happy; but there are a good many ways of serving God and doing one's duty; and if we try to serve him and to live for duty, it will all come out right at last. You will be a happier woman, Pauline, if you do it, than if you rebel against it, and try to find some other way, and put yourself in a subordinate place, or a place of dependence, and waste your life, and expose yourself to temptation. No, no, Pauline, I cannot see you do it. Heaven knows, I wish you had somebody else to direct you. But it has all come upon me, and I must do the best I can. I think any one else would advise the same, who had the same means of judging."

"I will do just what you think best," I said, almost in a whisper, getting up.

"That is right," he answered, in a husky voice, rising too, and putting my cloak about my shoulders, which had fallen off. "You will see it will be best."

CHAPTER XXII.

A GREAT DEAL TOO SOON.

But her sad eyes, still fastened on the ground,
Are governed with a goodly modesty,
That suffers not a look to glance away,
Which may let in a little thought unsound.

Spenser.

Vouloir ce que Dieu veut est la seule science
Qui nous met en repos.

Malherbe.

RICHARD had obtained for me (with difficulty), from the lawyer of the new uncle who had arisen, the privilege of remaining in the house for another month, undisturbed in any way. At the end of those four weeks I was to be married to him, one day, quietly in church, and to go away. It was very hard to have to see Sophie, and be treated with ignominy, for doing what I did not want to do; it was very hard to make preparations to leave the only place I wanted to stay in now; it was very hard to be tranquil and even, while my heart was like lead. But I had begun to discover that that was the general order of things here below, and it did not amaze me as it had done at first.

I was doing my duty, to the best of my discernment, and was not to be deterred by all the lead in the world.

It was very well for Richard to say, he did it for sacrifice and for duty. I have no doubt at first he did it greatly for those two things : but he grew happier every day, I could see. He was very considerate of my sadness, and always acted on the basis on which our engagement was begun, never keeping my hand in his, or kissing me, or asking any of the trifling favors of a lover.

He was grave and silent : but I could see the change in his face; I could see that he was more exacting of every moment that I spent away from him; he kept near me, and followed me with his eyes, and seemed never to be satisfied with his possession of me.

He bought me the most beautiful jewels, (he had made great strides toward fortune in the last six months, and was a rich man now in earnest,) and though he never clasped them on my throat or wrist, nor even fitted a ring on my finger, I could feel his eyes upon me, hungering for a smile, a word of gratitude.

And who would not have been grateful? But it was "too soon, a great deal too soon," as he had said himself. I was very grateful, but I would have been glad to die.

I have wondered whether he saw it or not. I rather think not. I was very submissive and gentle, and tried to be bright, and I think he was so absorbed in the satisfaction of my promise, so intent upon his plans for making me happy, and for making me love him, that he made himself believe there was no heart of lead below the tranquillity he saw.

It was the third week since my uncle's death. The next week was to come the marriage, on Wednesday, the 19th of May.

"Marriages in May are not hap y," said Ann Coddle.

"I did not need you to tell me that," I thought.

It was on Thursday, the 13th; Richard had come up a little earlier, in the evening. It grew to be a little earlier every evening.

"By-and-by he will not go down-town at all, at this rate," I said to myself, when I heard his ring that night.

I was sitting by the parlor-lamp, with the evening paper in my lap, of which I had not read a word. He came and sat down by the table, and we talked a little while. I tried to find things to talk about, and wondered if it always would be so. I felt as if some day I should give out entirely, and have to go through bankruptcy. (And take a fresh start.)

He never seemed to feel the want of talking; I suppose he was quite satisfied with his thoughts, and with having me beside him.

By-and-by, he said he should have to go up to the library, and look over the last of some books of my uncle's, and finish an inventory that he had begun. Could I not bring my work and sit there by him? I felt a little selfish, for we were already on the last week, and I said I thought I would sit in the parlor. I had to write a letter to Sister Madeline. I had not heard a word from her yet, though I had written twice.

Why could not I write in the library?

I always liked to be alone when I wrote letters: I could not think, when any one was in the room. Besides, trying to smile, he would be sure to talk.

He looked disappointed, and lingered a good while before he went away. As he rose to go away he threw into my lap a little package, saying,

" There is some white lace for you. Can't you use it on some of your clothes? I don't know anything about such things : maybe it isn't pretty enough, but I thought perhaps it would do for that lilac silk you talked of."

I opened the package : it was exquisite, fit for a princess; and as I bent over it, I thought, how dead I must be, that it gave me no pleasure to know it was my own, for I had loved such baubles so, a year ago.

"What a mass of it !" I exclaimed, unfolding yard on yard.

"You must always wear lace," he said, throwing one end of it over my black dress around the shoulder. "I like you in it. I am tired of those stiff little linen collars."

The lace had given me a little compunction about not spending the evening with him : but as I had said so, I could not draw back ; so I compromised the matter by going up to the library with him, to see that he was comfortable, before I came down to write my letter.

I brought the little student-lamp from my own room and lit it, and put it on the library-table, and brought him some fresh pens, and opened the inkstand for him, even pushed up the chair and put a little footstool by it. Though he was standing by the bookshelves, and seemed to be engrossed by them, I knew that he was watching me, filled with content and satisfaction.

"Do you remember where that box of cigars was

put?" he said, turning to me as I paused. That was to keep me longer; for they were on the shelf, half a yard from where he stood.

I got the cigar-box and put it on the table.

"Now you will want some matches, and this stand is almost empty." So I took it away with me to my room, and came back with it filled.

"Is there anything else that I can do?" I said, pausing as I put it on the table.

"No, Pauline. I believe not. Thank you."

I think that moment Richard was nearer to happiness than he had ever been before. Poor fellow!

I went down-stairs, feeling quite easy in mind, and sat down to my letter. That threw me back into the past, for to Sister Madeline I poured out my heart. An hour went by, and I had forgotten Richard and the library. I was recalled to the present by hearing some books fall on the floor (the library was over the parlor); and by hearing Richard's step heavily crossing the room. I started up, pushed my letter into my portfolio, and wiped away my tears, quite frightened that Richard should see me crying. To my surprise, he came hurriedly down the stairs, passed the parlor-door, opened the hall-door, and shutting it heavily after him, was gone, without a word to me. This startled me for a moment, it was so unusual. But my heart was not enough engaged to be wounded by the slight, and I very soon returned to my letter and my other thoughts.

When I went up to bed, I stopped in the library, and found the lamp still burning, the pens unused, a cigar, which had been lighted, but unsmoked, lying on the table. A book was lying on the floor at the foot of the bookshelf, where I had left Richard standing. I picked it up. "This was the last book that Uncle Leonard ever read," I said to myself, turning its pages over. I remembered that he had it in his hand the last night of his life, when I bade him goodnight. I was not in the room the next day, till he was brought home in a dying state.

Ann had put the books in order, and arranged them, after he went down-town in the morning.

I wondered whether Richard knew that that was the last book he had been reading, and I put it by, to tell him of it in the morning when he came. But in the morning Richard did not come. Unusual again; and I was for an hour or two surprised. He always found some excuse for coming on his way down-town: and it was very odd that he should not want to explain his sudden going away last night. But, as before, my lack of love made the wound very slight, and in a little time I had forgotten all about it, and was only thinking that this was Friday—and that Wednesday was coming very near.

CHAPTER XXIII.

All this is to be sanctified,
This rupture with the past;
For thus we die before our deaths,
And so die well at last.

Faber.

DINNER-time came, and passed, and still Richard did not come. At eight o'clock Ann brought the tea, as usual, and it stood nearly an hour upon the table; and then I told her to take it away.

By this time I had begun to feel uneasy. Something must have happened. It would necessarily be something uncomfortable, perhaps something that would frighten me, and give me another shock. And I dreaded that so; I had had so many. But perhaps, dreadful though it might be, it would bring me a release. Perhaps Richard was only angry with me, and *that* might bring me a release.

At nine o'clock I heard a ring at the bell, and then his step in the hall. He was slower than usual in coming in; everything made me feel confused and apprehensive. When he opened the door and entered, I was trying to command myself, but I forgot all about myself when I saw *him*. His face was white, and he looked haggard and harassed, as if he had gone through a year of suffering since last night, when I left him. with the lamp and cigar in the library.

I started up and put out my hand. "What is it, Richard? You are in some trouble."

He said no, and tried to speak in an ordinary tone, sitting down on the sofa by my chair.

I was confused and thrown back by this, and tried to talk as if nothing had been said.

"Will you have a cup of tea?" I asked; "Ann has just taken it away."

He said absently, yes, and I rang for Ann to bring the tea, and then went to the table to pour it out.

He sat with his face leaning on his hand on the arm of the sofa, and did not seem to notice me till I carried the cup to him, and offered it. Then he started, and looked up and took it, asking my pardon, and thanking me.

"Are you not going to have one yourself?" he said, half rising.

"No, I don't want any to-night. Tell me if yours is right."

"Yes, it is very nice," he said absently, drinking some. Then rising suddenly, he put the cup on the mantleshelf, and said to me, "Send Ann away, I want to talk to you."

I told Ann I would ring for her when I wanted her, and sat down by the lamp again, with many apprehensions.

"You asked me if anything had happened, Pauline, didn't you?" he said.

".No," I answered. "But I was sure that something had, from the way you looked when you came in."

"It is something that—that changes things very much for you, Pauline," he resumed, with an effort, "and makes all our arrangements unnecessary—that is, unless you choose."

I looked amazed and frightened, and he went on.

"I made a discovery last night in the library. The will is found, Pauline."

I started to my feet, with my hands pressed against my heart, waiting breathlessly for his next word.

"Everything is left to you—and I have come to tell you, you are free—if you desire to be."

"Oh, thank God! Thank God!" I cried; then covering my face with my hands, sank back into my seat, and burst into tears.

He turned from me and walked to the other end of the room; each of us lived much in that little time.

For myself, I had accepted my bondage so meekly, so dutifully, that I did not know the weight it had been upon me till it was suddenly taken off. I did not think of him—I could only think, there was no next Wednesday, and I could stay where I was. It was like the sudden cessation of dreadful and long-continued pain: it was Heaven. I was crying for joy. But at last the reaction came, and I had to think of him.

"Oh, Richard," I cried, going toward him, (he was sitting by the window, and his hand concealed his eyes.) "I don't know what you think of me, I hope you can forgive me."

He did not speak, and I felt a dreadful pang of self-reproach.

"Richard," I said, crying, and taking hold of his hand, "I am ashamed of myself for being glad. I will marry you yet, if you want me to. I know how good you have been to me. I know I am ungrateful and abominable."

Still he did not speak. His very lips were white, and his hand, when I touched it, did not meet mine or move.

"You are angry with me," I cried, bursting into a flood of tears. "Oh, how you ought to hate me. Oh,

·I wish'we had never seen each other. I wish I had been dead before I brought you all this trouble. Richard, do look at me—do speak to me. Don't you believe that I am sorry? Don't you know I will do anything you want me to?".

He seemed to try to speak—moved a little, as a person in pain might do, but, bending his head a little lower on his hand, was silent still.

"Richard," I said, after several moments' silence, speaking thoughtfully—"it has all come to me at last. I begin to see what you have been to me always, and how badly I have treated you. But it must have been because I was very young, and did not think. I am sure my heart was not so bad, and I mean to be different now. You know I have not had any one to teach me. Will you let me try and make you happy?"

"No, Pauline," he said at last, speaking with effort. "It is all over now, and we will never talk of it again."

I was silent for many minutes—standing before him with irresolution. "If it was right for me to marry you before," I said at last, "Why is it not right now, if I mean to do my duty?"

"No, it is no longer right, if it ever was," he answered. "I will not take advantage of your sense of duty now, as I was going to take advantage of your necessity before. No, you are free, and it is all at an end."

"You are unjust to yourself. You were not taking advantage of my necessity. You were saving me, and I am ashamed of myself when I think of everything. Oh, Richard, where did you learn to be so good!"

A spasm of pain crossed his face, and he turned away from me.

"If you give me up," I said timidly, "who will take care of me?"

"There will be plenty now," he answered bitterly.

"There wasn't anybody yesterday."

"But there will be to-morrow. No, Pauline," he said, lifting his head and speaking in a firmer voice, "What I thought I was doing, till this showed me my heart, and how I had deceived myself, I will do now, even if it kills me. I thought I was acting for your good, and from a sense of duty: now that I know what is for your good, and what is my duty, I will go on in that, and nothing shall turn me from it, so help me Heaven."

"At least you will forgive me," I said, with tears, "for all the things that I have made you suffer."

13

"Yes," he said, with some emotion, "I shall forgive you sooner than I shall forgive myself. I cannot see that you have been to blame."

"Ah," I cried, hiding my face with shame, when I thought of all my selfishness and indifference, and the return I had made him for his devoted love. "I know how I have been to blame; and I am going to pay you for your goodness and care by breaking your heart for you—by upsetting all your plans. Oh, Richard! You had better let it all go on! Think how everybody knows about it!"

He shook his head. "I don't care a straw for that," he said. And I am sure he did not.

"No," he said firmly, getting up, and walking up and down the room; "it is all over, and we must make the best of it. I shall still have everything to do for you under the will; and while you mustn't expect me to see you often, just for the present time, at least, you know I shall do everything as faithfully as if nothing had occurred. You must write to me whenever you think my judgment or advice would do you any good. And I shall be always looking after things that you don't understand, and taking care of your interests, whether you hear from me or not. You'll always be sure of that, whatever may occur."

"Oh," I faltered, with a sudden frightened feeling

of loneliness and loss, in the midst of my new free-dom, " I can't feel as if it were all over."

" I don't know how this terrible mistake about the will occurred," he went on, without noticing what I said : " it was only a—mercy that I found it when I did. It was between the leaves of a book, an old volume of Tacitus; I took it down to look at the title for the inventory, and it fell out."

" That was the book he had in his hand when I saw him last, that night before he died."

" Yes? Then after you went up-stairs I suppose he was thinking of you, and he took out the will to read it over, and maybe left it out, meaning to lock it up again in the morning."

" And in the morning he was not well," I said, " and perhaps went away leaving it lying on the book; I remember, Ann said there were several papers lying on the table, when she arranged the room."

" No doubt," said Richard, " she shut it up in the book it laid on, and put it on the shelf. But it is all one how it came about. The will is all correct and duly executed. One of the witnesses was a clerk, who returned yesterday from South America, where he had been gone for several months. The other is lying ill at his home in Westchester, but I have sent to-day and had his deposition taken.   It is all in order, and there can be no dispute."

I think at that moment I should have been glad if it had been found invalid.   There was something so inevitable and final in Richard's plain and practical words.

Evidently a great change had come in my life, and I could not help it if I would.   I could not but feel the separation from the person upon whom I had leaned so long, and who had done everything for me, and I knew this separation was to be a final one; Richard's words left no doubt of that.

"What you'd better do," he said, leaning by the mantelpiece, "is to tell the servants about this— this—change in your plans, to-morrow; unpack, and settle the house to stay here for the present.   In the course of a couple of months it will be time enough to make up your mind about where you will live.   I think, till the will is admitted and all that, you had better keep things as they are, and make no change."

He had been so used to thinking or me, that he could not give it up at once.   "I will tell Sophie to-morrow," he went on.   "It will not be necessary for you to see her if she should come before she hears of it from me." (Sophie had an engagement with me to

go out on the following morning. He seemed to
to have forgotten nothing.)

" What will Sophie think of me ? " I said, with my
eyes on the floor. "Richard, it looks very bad for
me; when I was poor, I was going to marry you,
and now that I have money left me, I am going to
break it off."

" What difference does it make how it looks," he
said, "when you know you have done right? I will
tell Sophie the truth, that it was my doing both
times, and that you only yielded to my judgment
in the matter. Besides, if she judges you harshly,
it need not make much matter to you. You will
never again be thrown intimately with her, I suppose."

" No, I suppose not," I said faintly. I was being
turned out of my world very fast, and it was not
very clear what I was going to get in exchange for
it (except freedom).

"I will send you up money to-morrow morning,"
he went on, "to pay the servants, and all that. The
clerk I shall send it by, is the one that I shall put in
charge of your matters. You can always draw on
him for money, or ask him any questions, or call on
him for any service, in case I should be away, or ill,
or anything."

"You are going away?" I said interrogatively.

"It is possible, for a while—I don't know. I haven't made up my mind definitely about what I am going to do. But in case I *should* be away, I mean, you are to call on him."

"I understand."

"Anything he tells you, about signing papers, and such things, you may be sure is all right."

"Yes."

"But don't do anything, without consulting me, for anybody else, remember."

"I'll remember," I said absently and humbly. It was no wonder Richard felt I needed somebody to take care of me!

"I believe there's nothing else I wanted to say to you," he said at last, moving from the mantelpiece where he had been standing; "at least, nothing that I can't write about, when it occurs to me."

"Oh, Richard!" I said, beginning to cry again, as I knew that the moment of parting had come, "I don't understand you at all. I think you take it very calm."

"Isn't that the way to take it?" he said, in a voice that was, certainly, very calm indeed.

I looked up in his face: he was ten years older. I really was frightened at the change in him.

"Oh!" I exclaimed, putting my face down in my hands, "I wasn't worth all I've made you suffer."

"Maybe you weren't," he said simply, "But it wasn't either, your fault or mine—and you couldn't help it—that I wanted you."

He made a quick movement as he passed the table, and my work-basket fell at his feet, and a little jewel-box rolled across the floor. It was a ring he had brought me, only three days before.

He stooped to pick it up, and I saw his features contract as if in pain, as he laid it back upon the table. And his voice was unsteady, as he said, not looking at me while he spoke,

"I hope you won't send any of these things back. If there's anything you're willing to keep, because I gave it to you, I'd like it very much. The rest send to your church, or somewhere. I don't want to have to look at them again."

By this time I was sobbing, and, sitting down by the table, had buried my face on my arms.

"I'm sorry that it makes you feel so," he said, "but it can't be helped. Don't cry, I can't bear to see you cry. Good-bye, Pauline; God bless you."

And he was gone. I did not realize it, and did not lift my head, till I heard the heavy sound of the outer door closing after him.

Then I knew it was all over, and that things were changed for me indeed.

"I cannot cry and get over it as you can," he had said.

And if tears would have got me over it, I should have been cured that night.

CHAPTER XXIV.

MY NEW WORLD.

Few are the fragments left of follies past;
For worthless things are transient. Those that last
Have in them germs of an eternal spirit,
And out of good their permanence inherit.

Bowring.

Nor they unblest,
Who underneath the world's bright vest
With sackcloth tame their aching breast,
The sharp-edged cross in jewels hide.

Keble.

From eighteen to twenty-four—a long step; and it covers the ground that is generally the brightest and gayest in a woman's life, and the most decisive. With me it was, in a certain sense, bright and gay ; but the deciding events of my life seemed to have been crowded into the year, the story of which has just been told. Of the six years that came after, there is not much to tell. My character went on forming itself, no doubt, and interiorly I was growing in one direction or the other; but in external matters, there is not much of interest.

I had "no end of money," so it seemed to me, and

13*

to a good many other people, I should think, from the way that they paid me court. I don't see why it did not turn my head, except that I was what they call religious, and dreadfully afraid of doing wrong. I was not my own mistress exactly, either, for I had some one to direct my conscience, though that was the only direction that I ever had. I had not the smallest restriction as to money from Richard (to whom the estate was left in trust); and it had been found much to exceed his expectations, or those of anybody else.

I had the whole world before me, where to go and what to choose; not very much stability of character, and the greatest ignorance; a considerable share of good looks, and the love of pleasure inseparable from youth and health; absolutely no authority, and any amount of flattery and temptation. I think it must be agreed, it was a happy thing for me that I was brought under the influence of Sister Madeline, and that through her I was made to feel most afraid of sin, and of myself; and that the life within, the growth in grace, and the keeping clear my conscience, was made to appear of more consequence than the life without, that was so full of pleasures and of snares.

I often think now of the obedience with which I

would give up a party, stay at home alone, and read a good book, because I had been advised to do it, or because it was a certain day; of the simplicity with which I would put away a novel, when its interest was at the height, because it was ˌthe hour for me to read something different, or because it was Friday, or because I was to learn to give up doing what I wanted to.

These things, trivial in themselves, and never bound upon my conscience, only offered as advice, had the effect of breaking up the constant influence of the world, giving me a little time for thought, and opportunity for self-denial. I cannot help thinking such things are very useful for young persons, and particularly those who have only ordinary force and resolution. At least, I think they were made a means of security to me. I was so in earnest to do right, that I often thought, in terror for myself, in the midst of alluring pleasures and delights, it was a pity they had not let me be a Sister when I wanted to at first. (I really think I had more vocation than they thought: I could have *given up*, to the end of life, without a murmur, if that is what is necessary.) As to the people who wanted to marry me, I did not care for any of them, and seemed to have much less coquetry than of old. They simply did not interest me, (of course,

in a few years, I had outgrown the love that I had
supposed to be so immortal.) It was very pleasant to be
always attended to, and to have more constant homage
than any other young woman whom I saw. But as
to liking particularly any of the men themselves, it
never occurred to me to think of it.

I was placed by my fortunate circumstances rather
above the intrigue, and detraction, and heart-burning,
that attends the social struggle for life in ordinary
cases. If I were envied, I did not know it, and I
had small reason to envy anybody else, being quite
the queen.

I enjoyed above measure, the bright and pleasant
things that I had at my command: the sunny rooms
of my pretty house: the driving, the sailing, the
dancing: all that charms a healthy young taste, and
is innocent. I took journeys, with the ecstasy of
youth and of good health. I never shall forget the
pleasure of certain days and skies, and the enjoyment
that I had in nature. In society, I had a little more
weariness, as I grew older, and found a certain want
of interest, as was inevitable. Society isn't all made
up of clever people, and even clever people get to be
tiresome in the course of time. But at twenty-four I
was by no means *blasé*, only more addicted to books
and journeys, and less enthusiastic about parties

and croquet, though these I could enjoy a little yet.

I had a pretty house (and re-furnished it very often, which always gave me pleasure). I had no care, for Richard had arranged that I should have a very excellent sort of person for duenna, who had a good deal of tact, and didn't bore me, and was shrewd enough to make things very smooth. I liked her very much, though I think now she was something of a hypocrite. But she had enough principle to make things very respectable, and I never took her for a friend. We had very pretty little dinners, and little evenings when anybody wanted them, though the house wasn't very large. My duenna (by name Throckmorton) liked journeys as well as I did, and never objected to going anywhere. Altogether we were very comfortable.

The people whom I had known in that first year of my social existence, had drifted away from me a good deal in this new life. Sophie I could not help meeting sometimes, for she was still a gay woman, but I naturally belonged to a younger set, and did not go very long into general society. We still disliked each other with the cordiality of our first acquaintance, but I was very sorry for it, and had a great many repentances about it after every meeting. Kilian I met a good deal, but we rather avoided each other, at short range, though exceedingly good friends to the general observation.

Mary Leighton I seldom saw; no doubt she was consumed with envy when she heard of me, for they were poor, and not able to keep up with gay life as would have pleased her. She still maintained her intimacy with Kilian, for he had not the resolution to break off a flirtation of which, I was sure, he must be very tired.

Henrietta had married very well, two years after I saw her at R——, and was the staid, placid matron that she was always meant to be.

Charlotte Benson was the clever woman still: a little stronger-minded, and no less good-looking than of old, and no more. People were beginning to say that she would not marry, though she was only twenty-six. She did not go much to parties, and was not in my set. She affected art and lectures, and excursions to mountains, and campings-out, and unconventionalities, and no doubt had a good time in her way. But it was not my way: and so we seldom met. When we did, she did not show much more respect for me than of old, which always had the effect of making me feel angry.

And as for Richard, we could not have been much

further apart, if he had lived "in England and I at Rotterdam." For a year, while he was settling up the estate, he was closely in the city. I did not see him more than once or twice, all business being transacted through his lawyer, and the clerk of whom he had spoken to me. After the business matters of the estate were all in order, he went away, intending, I believe, to stay a year or two. But he came back before many months were over, and settled down into the routine of business life, which now seemed to have become necessary to him.

Travel was only a weariness to him in his state of mind; and work, and city-life, seemed the panacea. He did not live with Sophie, but took apartments, which he furnished plainly; and seemed settling down, according to his brother, into much of the sort of life that Uncle Leonard had led so many years in Varick-street.

Sophie still went to R——, and I often heard of the pleasant parties there in summer. But Richard seldom went, and seemed to have lost his interest in the place, though I have no doubt he spent more money on it than before. I heard of many improvements every year.

And Richard was now a man of wealth, so much so that people talked about him; and the newspapers said, in talking about real-estate, or investments, or institutions of charity—"When such men as Richard Vandermarck allow their names to appear, we may be sure," etc., etc. He was now the head of the firm, and one of the first business men of the city. He seemed a great deal older than he was; thirty-seven is young to occupy the place he held.

Such a *parti* could not be let alone entirely. His course was certainly discouraging, and it needs tough hopes to live on nothing. But stranger things had happened; more obdurate men had yielded; and un-appropriated loveliness hoped on. The story of an early attachment was afloat in connection with his name. I don't know whether I was made to play a part in it or not.

I saw him, perhaps, twice a year, not oftener. His manner was always, to me, peculiarly grave and kind; to every one, practical and unpretending. I had many letters from him, particularly when I was away on journeys. He seemed always to want to know exactly where I was, and to feel a care of me, though his letters never went beyond business matters, and advice about things I did not understand.

As my guardian, he could not have done less, nor was it necessary that he should do more; still I often wished it would occur to him to come and see me oftener, and give me an opportunity of showing him how much I had improved, and how different I had become. I had the greatest respect for his opinion; and he had grown, unconsciously to myself, to be a sort of oracle with me, and a sort of hero, too.

I was apt to compare other men with him, and they fell very far short of his measure in my eyes. That may have been because I saw him much too seldom, and the other men much too often.

CHAPTER XXV.

Keep, therefore, a true woman's eye,
And love me still, but know not why;
So hast thou the same reason still
To doat upon me ever!

"It' svery nice to be at home again," I said to Mrs. Throckmorton, as I broke a great lump of coal in pieces, and watched the flames with pleasure.

"Yes," said Mrs. Throckmorton, putting another piece of sugar in her coffee, for she was still at the table. "That is, if you call this home; I must confess it doesn't feel so to me altogether."

"Well, it's our own dear, noisy, raging, racketing, bustling old city, if it isn't our own house, and I'm sure we're very comfortable."

"Very," said Mrs. Throckmorton, who was always pleased.

"Every time I hear the tinkle of a car-bell, or the roar of an omnibus, I feel a thrill of pleasure," I said; "I never was so glad to get anywhere before."

" That's something new, isn't it?" said Mrs. Throckmorton, briefly.

" I don't know; I think I am always glad to get back home."

" And very glad to go away again too, my dear."

"I don't think I shall travel any more," I returned. " The fact is, I am getting too old to care about it, I believe."

Mrs. Throckmorton laughed, being considerably over forty, and still as fond of going about as ever.

We were only *de retour* two days. We had started eighteen months ago, for at least three years in Europe, and I had found myself unaccountably tired of it at the end of a year and a half; and here we were.

Our house was rented, but that I had not allowed to be any obstacle, though Mrs. Throckmorton, who was very well satisfied with the easy life abroad, had tried to make it so. I had secured apartments which were very pretty and complete. We had found them in order, and we had come there from the steamer. I was eminently happy at being where I wanted to be.

" How odd it seems to be in town and have nobody know it," I said, thinking, with a little quiet satisfaction, how pleased several people I could name would be, if they only knew we were so near them.

"Nobody but Mr. Vandermarck, I suppose," said Mrs. Throckmorton.

"Not even he," I answered, "for he can't have got my letter yet; it was only mailed the day we started. It was only a chance, you know, our getting those staterooms, and we were in such a hurry. I was so much obliged to that dear, old German gentleman for dying. We shouldn't have been here if he hadn't."

"Pauline, my dear!"

"Well, I can't think, as he's probably in heaven, that he can have begrudged us his tickets to New York."

"I should think not," said Mrs. Throckmorton, with a little sigh. For New York was not heaven to her, and she had spent a good deal of the day in looking up the necessary servants for our establishment, which, little as it was, required just double the number that had made us comfortable abroad.

She had too much discretion to trouble me with her cares, however, so she said cheerfully, after a few moments, by way of diverting my mind and her own—

"Well, I heard some news to-day."

"Ah!"—(I had been unpacking all day; and Mrs. Throckmorton in the interval of servant-hunting had not been able to refrain from a visit or two, *en passant*, to dear friends.)

"Yes: Kilian Vandermarck was married yesterday."

"Yesterday! how odd. And pray, who has he married? Not Mary Leighton, I should hope."

"Leighton. Yes, that's the name. No money, and a little *passé*. Everybody wonders."

"Well, he deserves it. That is even-handed justice. I'm not sorry for him. He's been trifling all his days, and now he's got his punishment. It serves Sophie right, too. I know she can't endure her. She never thought there was the slightest danger. But I'm sorry for Richard, that he's got to have such a girl related to him."

"Oh, well," said Mrs. Throckmorton, "I don't know whether that'll affect him very much, for they say he's going to be married too."

"Richard!"

"Yes; and to that Benson girl, you know."

"Who told you?"

"Mary Ann. She's heard it half a dozen times, she says. I believe it's rather an old affair. His sister made it up, I'm told. The young lady's been spending the summer with them, and this autumn it came out."

"I don't believe it."

"I'm sure I don't know; only that's the talk. It would be odd, though, if we'd just come home in time for the wedding.   You'll have to give her something handsome, being your guardian, and all."

I wouldn't give her anything, and she shouldn't marry Richard, I thought, as I leaned back in my chair and looked into the fire; a great silence having fallen on us since the delivery of that piece of news.

I said I didn't believe it, and yet I'm afraid I did. It was so like a man to give in at last; at least, like any man but Richard.   He had always liked Charlotte Benson, and known how clever she was, and Sophie had been so set upon it, (particularly since Richard had had so much money that he had given her a handsome settlement that nothing would affect.) And now that Kilian was married and would have the place, unless Richard wanted it, it was natural that Sophie should approve Richard having *his* wife there instead of Kilian having his; Kilian's being one that nobody particularly approved.

Yes, it did sound very much like probability.   I wasn't given to self-analysis; but I acknowledged to myself, that I was very much disappointed, and that if I had known that this was going to happen, I should have stayed in Europe.

I had never felt as if there were any chance of Richard marrying any one; I had not said to myself, that his love for me still had an existence, nor had I any reason to believe it. But the truth had been, I had always felt that he belonged to me, and was my right, and I felt a bitter resentment toward this woman, who was supposed to have usurped my place. How *dared* Richard love anybody else! I was angry with him, and very much hurt, and very, very unhappy.

Long after Mrs. Throckmorton went to her middle-aged repose, I sat up and went through imaginary scenes, and reviewed the situation a hundred times, and tried to convince myself of what I wanted to believe, and ended without any satisfaction.

One thing was certain. If Richard was going to marry Charlotte Benson, he was not going to do it because he loved her. He might not be prevented from doing it because he loved me ; but he did not love her. I could not say why exactly. But I knew she was not the kind of woman for him to think of loving, and I would not believe it till I heard it from himself, and I would hear it from himself at the earliest possible date. I did not like to be unhappy, and was very impatient to get rid of this, if it were not true, and to know the worst, at once, if it were.

"My dear Throcky," I said to my companion, at the breakfast-table, "I think you'd better go and take dinner with your niece to-day. I've sent for Mr. Van-

dermarck to come and dine, and I thought perhaps
you'd rather not be bored; we shall have business to
talk about, and business is such a nuisance when
you're not interested in it."

"Very well, my dear," said Mrs. Throckmorton,
with indestructible good-humor.

"Or you might have a headache, if you'd rather,
and I'll send your dinner up to you. I'll be sure
Susan takes you everything that's nice."

"Well, then, I think I'll have a headache; I'm
afraid I'd rather have it than one of Mary Ann's poor
dinners. (I'd be sure of one to-morrow if I went.)"

"Paris things have spoiled you, I'm afraid," I said.
"Only see that I have something nice for Richard,
won't you?—How do you think the cook is going
to do?" This was the first sign of interest I had given
in the matter of *ménage;* by which it will be seen I
was still a little selfish, and not very wise. But
Throckmorton was a person to cultivate my selfishness, and there had not been much to develop the
wisdom of common life.

She promised me a very pretty dinner, no matter at
what trouble, and made me feel quite easy about her
wounded feelings. One of the best features of Throckmorton was, she hadn't any feelings; you might treat
her like a galley-slave, and she would show the least

dejection. It was a temptation to have such a person in the house.

I had sent a note to Richard which contained the following:

"DEAR RICHARD:

"I am sure you will be surprised to know we have returned. But the fact is, I got very tired of Italy; and we were disappointed in the apartments we wanted in Berlin, and some of the people we expected to have with us had to give it up, and altogether it seemed dull, and we thought it would be just as pleasant to come home. We were able to get staterooms that just suited us, and it didn't seem worth while to lose them by waiting to send word. We had a very comfortable voyage, and I am glad to find myself at home, though Mrs. Throckmorton doesn't think the rooms are very nice. I want to know if you won't come to dinner. We dine at six. Send a line back by the boy. I want to ask you about some business matters.

"Affectionately yours,

"PAULINE."

And I had received for answer:

"MY DEAR PAULINE:

"Of course I am astonished to think you are at home.

14 ·

I enclosed you several letters by the steamer yesterday, none of them of any very great importance,
though, I think.   I will come up at six.

        " Always yours,

                " RICHARD VANDERMARCK.

"P. S.   I am very glad you wanted to come home."

I read this letter over a great many times, but it did
not enlighten me at all as to his intentions about
marrying Charlotte Benson.   It was very matter-of-
fact, but that Richard's letters always were.   Evidently he had thought the same of it himself, as he
read it over, and had added the postscript.   But that
did not seem very enthusiastic.   Altogether I was not
happy, waiting for six o'clock to come.

CHAPTER XXVI.

A DINNER.

Time and chance are but a tide,
Slighted love is sair to bide.

THE dining-room and parlor of our little suite adjoined; the door was standing open between them, as I walked up and down the parlor, waiting nervously for Richard to arrive. The fire was bright, and the only light in the parlor was a soft, pretty lamp, which we had brought from Italy. There were flowers on the table, and in two or three vases, and the curtains were pretty, and there were several large mirrors. Outside, it was the twilight of a dark autumnal day; almost night already, and the lamps were lit. It lacked several minutes of six when Richard came. I felt very much agitated when he entered the room. It was a year and a half since I had seen him : besides, this piece of news! But he looked just the same as ever, and I had not the self-possession to note whether he seemed agitated at meeting me. I do not know exactly what we talked about for the first few moments, probably I was occupied in trying to excuse myself for coming home so suddenly, for I found Richard was not altogether pleased at not having been informed, and thought there must be something yet to tell. He was not used to feminine caprice, and I began to feel a good deal ashamed of myself. I had to remind myself, more than once, that I was not responsible to any one.

"I just felt like it," was such a very weak explanation to offer to this grave business-man, for disarranging two years of carefully-laid plans.

I found I was getting to be a little afraid of Richard: we had been so long apart, and he had grown so much older.

"I hope, at least, you are not going to scold me for it," I said at last, with a little laugh, feeling that was my best way out of it. "I shall think you are not glad to see me."

"I am glad to see you," he said, gravely; "and as to scolding, it's so long since you've given me an opportunity, I should not know how to go to work."

"Do you mean, because I've been away so long, or because I've been so good?"

Susan, who had been watching her opportunity, now appeared in the dining-room door, and said that dinner was on the table.

Richard asked for Mrs. Throckmorton when we sat down to dinner. I told him she was dining with her niece. (She had reconsidered the question of the headache, and had gone to hear more news.) The dinner was very nice, and very nicely served; but somehow, Richard did not seem to enjoy it very much, that is, not as I had been in the habit lately of seeing men enjoy their meals.

"I am afraid you are getting like Uncle Leonard, and only care about Wall-street," I said. "I shouldn't wonder if you forgot to order your dinner half the time, and took the same thing for breakfast every morning in the year."

"That's just exactly how it is," he said. "If Sophie did not come down to my quarters every week or two, and regulate affairs a little, I don't know where I should be, in the matter of my dinners."

"How is Sophie?" I said.

"Very well. I saw her yesterday. I went to put Charley in College for her."

"I can't think of Charley as a young man."

"Yes, Charley is a strapping fellow, within two inches of my height."

"Impossible! And where is Benny?"

"At school here in town. His mother will not let

him go to boarding-school. He is a nice boy : I think
there's more in him than Charley."

" And I hear Kilian is married !"

" Yes. Kilian is married—the very day you
landed, too."

" Well," I said, with a little dash of temper, " I'm
very sorry for you all. I did not think Kilian was
going to be so foolish."

" He thinks he's very wise, though, all the same,"
said Richard, with a smile, which turned into a sigh
before he had done speaking.

" I do dislike her so," I exclaimed, warmly. " There
isn't an honest or straightforward thing about her.
She is weak, too ; her only strength is her suppleness
and cunning."

" I know you never liked her," said Richard,
gravely ; " but I hope you'll try to think better of
her now."

" I hope I shall never have to see her," I answered,
with angry warmth.

Richard was silent, and I was very much ashamed
of myself a moment after. I had meant him to see
how much improved I was, and how well disciplined.
This was a pretty exhibition ! I had not spoken so
of any one for a year, at least. I colored with
mortification and penitence. Richard evidently

saw it, and felt sorry for me, for he said, most kindly,

"I can understand exactly how you feel, Pauline. This marriage is a great trial to me. I have done all I could to keep Kilian from throwing himself away, but I might as well have argued with the winds."

"I don't care how much Kilian throws himself away," I said, impulsively. "He deserves it for keeping around her all these years. But I do mind that she is your sister, and that she will be mistress of the house at R——."

There was an awful silence then. Heavens! what had I been thinking about to have said that! I had precipitated the *dénouement*, and I had not meant to. I did not want to hear it that moment, if he were going to marry Charlotte Benson, nor did I want to hear it, if he were saving the old place for me. I felt as if I had given the blow that would bring the whole structure down, and I waited for the crash in frightened silence.

In the meantime the business of the table went on. I ate half a chicken croquette, and Susan placed the salad before Richard, and another plate. He did not speak till he had put the salad on his plate; then he said, without looking at me, in a voice a good deal lower than was usual to him,

"She is not to be mistress of that house. They will live in town."

Then I felt cold and chilled to my very heart; it was well that he did not expect me to speak, for I could not have commanded my voice enough to have concealed my agitation. I knew very well from that moment that he was going to marry Charlotte Benson. Something that was said a little later was a confirmation.

I had recovered myself enough to talk about ordinary things, and to keep strictly to them, too. Richard was talking of the great heat of the past summer. I had said it had been unparalleled in France; had he not found it very uncomfortable here in town?

"I have been out of town so much, I can hardly say how it has been here," he answered. "I was all of August in the country; only coming to the city twice."

My heart sank: that was just what they had said; he had been a great deal at home this summer, and she had been there all the time.

The dinner was becoming terribly *ennuyant*, and I wished with all my heart Throckmorton had been contented with just half the courses. Richard did not seem to enjoy them, and I—I was so wretched I could scarcely say a word, much less eat a morsel. It had been a great mistake to invite him to take dinner ; it was being too familiar, when he had put me at such a distance all these years : I wished for Mrs. Throckmorton with all my heart. Why had I sent her off? Richard was evidently so constrained, and it was in such bad taste to have asked him here ; it could not help putting thoughts in both our minds, sitting alone at a table opposite each other, as we should have been sitting daily if that horrid will had not been found. He had dined with us just twice before, but that was at dinner-parties, when there had been ever so many people between us, and when I had not said six words to him during the whole evening.

The only excuse I could offer, and that he could understand, would be that I wanted to talk business to him ; I had said in my note that I wanted to consult him about something, and I must keep that in mind. I had wanted to ask him about a house I thought of buying, adjoining the Sisters' Hospital, to enlarge their work ; but I was so wicked and worldly, I felt just then as if I did not care whether they had a house or not, or whether they did any work. However, I resolved to speak about it, when we had got away from the table, if we ever did.

Susan kept bringing dish after dish.

" Oh, we don't want any of that !" I exclaimed, at

14*

last, impatiently; "do take it away, and tell them to send in the coffee."

I was resolved upon one thing: Richard should tell me of his engagement before he went away; it would be dishonorable and unkind if he did not, and I should make him do it. I was not quite sure that I had self-control enough not to show how it made me feel, when it came to hearing it all in so many words. But in very truth, I had not much pride as regarded him; I felt so sore-hearted and unhappy, I did not care much whether he knew it or suspected it.

I could not help remembering how little conceal-ment he had made of his love for me, even when he knew that all the heart I had was given to another. I would be very careful not to precipitate the disclos-ure, however, while we sat at table; it is so disagree-able to talk to any one on an agitating subject *vis-à-vis* across a little dinner-table, with a bright light over-head, and a servant walking around, able to stop and study you from any point she pleases.

Coffee came at last, though even that, Susan was unwilling to look upon as the legitimate finale, and had her views about liqueur, instructed by Throck-morton. But I cut it short by getting up and saying,

"I'm sure you'll be glad to go into the parlor; it gets warm so soon in these little rooms."

The parlor was very cool and pleasant; a window had been open, and the air was fresh, and the flowers were delicious, and the lamp was softer and pleasanter than the gas. I went to break up the coal and make the fire blaze, and Richard to shut the window down.

When I had pulled a chair up to the fire and seated myself, he stood leaning on the mantelpiece, on the other side from me. I felt sure he meant to go, the minute that he could get away—a committee meeting, no doubt, or some such nauseous fraud. But he should not go away until he had told me, that was certain.

"What is it that you wanted to ask me about, Pauline?" he said, rather abruptly.

My heart gave a great thump; how could he have known? Oh, it was the business that I had spoken of in my stupid note. Yes; and I began to explain to him what I wanted to do about the hospital.

He looked infinitely relieved. I believe he had an idea it was something very different. My explanation could not have added much to his reverence for my business-ability. I was very indefinite, and could not tell him whether it was hundreds or thousands that I meant.

He said, with a smile, he thought it must be thousands, as city property was so very high. He was very kind, however, about the matter, and did not discour-

age me at all. He always seemed to approve of my
desire to give away in charity, and, within bounds,
always furthered such plans of doing good. He said
he would look into it, and would write me word next
week what his impression was; and then, I think, he
meant to go away.

Then I began talking on every subject I could
think of, hoping some of the roads would lead to
Rome. But none of them led there, and I was in
despair.

" Oh, don't you want to look at some photographs ? "
I said, at last, thinking I saw an opening for my wedge.
I got the package, and he came to the table and looked
at them, standing up. They were naturally of much
more interest to me than to him, being of places and
people with which I had so lately been familiar.

But he looked at them very kindly, and asked a
good many questions about them.

" Look at this," I said, handing him an Antwerp
peasant-woman in her hideous bonnet. "Isn't that
ridiculously like Charlotte Benson ? I bought it because it was so singular a resemblance."

. " It is like her," he said, thoughtfully, looking at it
long. " The mouth is a little larger and the eyes
further apart. But it is a most striking likeness. It
might almost have been taken for her."

" How is she, and when have you seen her ?" I said, a little choked for breath.

" She is very well. I saw her yesterday," he answered, still looking at the little picture.

" Was she with Sophie this summer ?"

" Yes, for almost two months."

" I hope she doesn't keep everybody in order as sharply as she used to ?" I said, with a bitter little laugh.

" I don't know," he said. " I think, perhaps, she is rather less decided than she used to be."

" Oh, you call it decision, do you ? Well, I'm glad I know what it is. I used to think it hadn't such a pretty name as that."

Richard looked grave ; it certainly was not a graceful way to lead up to congratulations.

" But then, you always liked her," I said.

- " Yes, I always liked her," he answered, simply.

" I'm afraid I'm not very amiable," I retorted, " for I never liked her: no better even than that fraudulent Mary Leighton, clever and sensible as she always was. There is such a thing as being too clever, and too sensible, and making yourself an offence to all less admirable people."

Richard was entirely silent, and, I was sure, was disapproving of me very much.

"Do you know what I heard yesterday?" I said, in a daring way. "And I hope you're going to tell me if it's true, to-night?"

"What was it that you heard yesterday?" he asked, without much change of tone. He had laid down the photograph, and had gone back, and was leaning by the mantelpiece again.

"Why, I heard that you were going to marry Charlotte Benson. Is it true?"

I had pushed away the pile of photographs from me, and had looked up at him when I began, but my voice and courage rather failed before the end, and my eyes fell. There was a silence—a silence that seemed to stifle me.

"Why do you ask me that question?" he said, at last, in a low voice. "Do you believe I am, yourself?"

"No," I cried, springing up, and going over to his side. "No, I don't believe it. Tell me it isn't true, and promise me you won't ever, ever marry Charlotte Benson."

The relief was so unspeakable that I didn't care what I said, and the joy I felt showed itself in my face and voice. I put out my hand to him when I said "promise me," but he did not take it, and turned his head away from me.

"I shall not marry Charlotte Benson," he said; "but I cannot understand what difference it makes to you."

It was now my turn to be silent, and I shrank back a step or two in great confusion.

He raised his head, and looked steadily at me for a moment, and then said:

"Pauline, you did a great many things, but I don't think you ever willingly deceived me. Did you?"

I shook my head without looking up.

"Then be careful what you do now, and let the past alone," he said, and his voice was almost stern.

I trembled, and turned pale.

"Women sometimes play with dangerous weapons," he said; "I don't accuse you of meaning to give pain, but only of forgetting that some recollections are not to you what they are to me. I never want to interfere with any one's comfort or enjoyment; I only want to be let alone. I do very well, and am not unhappy. About marrying, now or ever, I should have thought you would have known. But let me tell you once for all: I haven't any thought of it, and shall not ever have. It is not that I am holding to any foolish hopes. It would be exactly the same if you were married, or had died. It simply isn't in my nature to feel the same way a second time. People are made differently, that is all. I'm very well contented, and you need never let it worry you."

He was very pale now, and his eyes had an expression I had never seen in them before.

"Richard," I said, faintly, "I never *have* deceived you: believe me now when I tell you, I am sorry from my heart for all that's past."

"You told me so before, and I did forgive you. I forgave you fully, and have never had a thought that wasn't kind."

"I know it," I said. "But you do not trust me— you don't ever come near me, or want to see me."

"You do not know what you are talking of," he answered, turning from me. "I forgive you anything you may have done at any time to give me pain. I will do everything I can to serve you, in every way I can; only do not stir up the past, and let me forget the little of it that I can forget."

I burst into tears, and put my hands before my face.

"What is it?" he said, uneasily. "You need not be troubled about me."

Seeing that I did not stop, he said again, "Tell me: is it that that troubles you?"

I shook my head.

"What is it, then? Something that I do not know

about? Pauline, you are unhappy, and yet you've everything in the world to make you happy. I often think, there are not many women have as much."

"The poorest of them are better off than I," I said, without raising my head.

"Then you are ungrateful," he said, "for you have youth, and health, and money, and everybody likes you. You could choose from all the world."

"No, I couldn't," I exclaimed, like a child; "and everybody doesn't like me,"—and then I cried again, for I was really in despair, and thought he meant to put me away, memory and all.

"Well, if that's your trouble," he said, with a sigh, "I suppose I cannot help you; but I'm very sorry."

"Yes, you *can* help me," I cried imploringly, forgetting all I ought to have remembered; "if you only would forgive me, really and in earnest, and be friends again—and let me try—" and I covered my face with my hands.

"Pauline," he said, standing by my side, and his voice almost frightened me, it was so strong with feeling; "is this a piece of sentiment? Do you mean anything? Or am I to be trifled with again?"

He took hold of my wrists with both his hands, with such force as to give me pain, and drew them from my face.

"Look at me," he said, "and tell me what you mean ; and decide now—forever and forever. For this is the last time that you will have a chance to say."

"It's all very well," I said, trying to turn my face away from him. "It's all very well to talk about loving me yet, and being just the same ; but this isn't the way you used to talk, and I think it's very hard—"

"That isn't answering me," he said, holding me closer to him.

"What shall I say," I whispered, hiding my face upon his arm. "Nothing will ever satisfy you."

"Nothing ever *has* satisfied me," he said, "—before."

THE END.